Remember the Constable?

West Riding Constabulary
Keighley Addingham Bolton Abbey
60s-70s

By Ken Pickles

Peacock Press

West Riding Constabulary
© Ken Pickles

ISBN 978-1-912271-13-9

Published by Peacock Press, 2017
Scout Bottom Farm
Mytholmroyd
Hebden Bridge HX7 5JS (UK)

Front and back cover photograph: Beamsley Beacon from Addingham
All photographs © Ken Pickles except where stated

Design and artwork by D&P Design and Print
Printed by Lightning Source UK

Remember the
Constable?

West Riding Constabulary

Keighley Addingham Bolton Abbey

60s-70s

By

Ken Pickles

Contents

DEDICATION

This book is written out of respect for and dedicated to those West Riding men I served with: Chief Superintendent Scowen Crawford Mogg ex pilot RAF, Chief Inspector Eric Dixon Captain, Duke of Wellington's Regt, Chief Inspector Harold Weaver Royal Navy (once Riddlesden Bobbie),Sgt Tom Haigh ex-Army, Sgt Tom Chapman ex RAF, Sgt Harry Spedding ex-Army, Barrie Shaw, Editor of White Rose and my wife Catherine the unsung hero who held the fort when I was on patrol and did much for the image of the police in handling public callers at all hours.

Introduction

This is a story of Policing in the West Riding of Yorkshire, firstly in a mill town called Keighley in the 60s when such towns were being hastily flattened to make way for structures worse than those destroyed then, after three years, in Wharfedale, a place of idyllic splendour but with its own problems.

The men who policed Keighley and district were mostly ex-servicemen, either National Service or WW2 veterans. They wanted a better country where crime and its attendant bad behaviour were reduced to a minimum. They had taken an Oath to serve the Queen and her people and worked selflessly to that end.

This beat system of policing had existed in Britain from the 1850s until the 1980s. The stories herein are not sensational for ordinary policing was about ordinary people. For a start police officers lived among the people they policed, were well known to them, respected and trusted by them and available to assist with every kind of problem; much that would not be considered a police matter today but it was that contact that made the long-tried system work.

Sir Robert Peel had his ideas extended to the counties in the midst of Queen Victoria's reign. He was a far-seeing man; an ordinary man for a politician; ordinary like the men who now wore the blue uniform and kept the peace. The ancient office of constable was revived and most villages had one. It was rare for any to have been to university although a few had attended the Royal Military College, Sandhurst, quickly creamed off to be instructors or guided onto the promotion ladder. The industrial towns had many constables to work the beats and keep them safe and law-abiding. In the newspaper adverts for recruits they were clearly after supermen and we were never that.

These recollections touch on a variety of incidents that occurred as I learned my trade. They are written to remind the people what was lost in the haste to modernise, to introduce graduates to run the police force who, because they had an 'ology' might just be the sort of people to keep the show on the road.

The working uniform now worn hardly commands respect and like the nylon shirts tried years ago cannot be very healthy. Smartness does matter but on the rare sightings today's police cannot be distinguished from council workmen, lollypop ladies or traffic wardens.

Undoubtedly, terrorism during the Irish troubles and since because of Britain's intervention in foreign wars has meant new ways of thinking. The retirement of most of those who served during WW2 seemed to remove the backbone from the service and in the 70s led to massive changes and the days of the beat constables was numbered.

Those men who did live among us have gone; no more the familiar sight patrolling the streets and none of us feel any safer for the change. Some look for the causes. Was it the treatment by the politicians of the miners in the 80s; was it, perhaps, the police's over concern with its own image and professionalism and less with a service to the British public? Personal experiences point to the lacklustre attitude of certain officers. Was this a general malaise or just individual idleness, for men questioned were clearly not happy with their work and wanted out! One serving officer described the present system as 'broken'! Now that is serious indeed and on the evidence it does appear to be the case or was it simply the quality of leadership of such a large amalgamated organisation? The larger a thing becomes whether a school, a hospital, an army or a police force the less easy it is to control and govern.

The idea of a police Sandhurst-like establishment called Bramshill seemed a good idea for preparing officers for specialist tasks and some of those have been very good who have gone through that system and reached senior rank but others do leave me wondering when I see them interviewed on television!

When I joined, many of us were still on the paid army reserve and that esprit de corps permeated our work and was a definite asset to the police service providing the discipline that would not countenance failure in the daily problems and it was rare indeed to discover an officer who was 'bent'! Perhaps we were a different breed, having lived through a world war, being brought up to serve, attending Sunday School, glad to help others from Scout example, immersed in the Ten Commandments on which all law is based, respectful of others, especially the elderly, and proud of our country and that Police tradition to which we then belonged. Our history and that of our wives and families had been well checked out and there were many restrictions on our private lives which we accepted.

The main thing perhaps was we had the respect of the public, even those who broke the law knew they would be treated fairly. The tall helmet and guardsman-like uniform was perhaps a little imposing and the psychological advantages of that, presence and height was understood.

Well, here is an outline of how it was and you must judge for yourself. We all dream of a world where we don't need soldiers to fight wars and policemen to keep the peace but we are not there yet. So remember with amusement, a little affection and some pride part of the British police force that for a time was the envy of the world.

Chapter 1

The Worth Valley and Me

Keighley had not always had that air of dereliction about it. In May, 1945, as a young boy I stood in the Town Hall Square before the war memorial as the smart soldiers of the Durham Light Infantry marched in to commemorate the end of World War Two. The town was a proud place then, with good proud people and fine architectural buildings now being ripped down along with the back-to-back cottages of the working people; people who had brought prosperity to the wealthy mill owners who were forgetting who had given them their wealth.

There seemed to be no vision. So much was worth keeping, the houses for instance were built of local stone and two could so easily have been made into one with every modern convenience. For the locals it seemed their own people and councillors were doing the work the Nazis failed to do. For the destruction of their homes some householders were receiving £50 compensation from the council after paying mortgages for half a lifetime. Now they were being rehoused in high-rise flats far from the places they knew. Many of these families could trace their ancestry back a thousand years or more as small-time landowners and hand-loom weavers prior to the industrial revolution.

Many descendants of Irish and Scottish stock had lived in the town since the 1850s following the famine which did not just affect Ireland. They had married into local stock and were indistinguishable from them. The only 'foreigners' I knew were a handful of evacuees from London who spoke with a cockney accent. Then there were the refugees from WW2, Poles, Latvians, Lithuanians, and Ukrainians. Apart from their accents and their names they were identical with us and they too married into the indigenous stock. They harmonised and adopted the Yorkshire dialect and customs and were an asset to the work force, glad to live in a country where there was freedom of speech and they were treated as equals.

Speaking particularly of the Irish mostly quartered in the area of West Lane and the Pinfold prior to absorption into the wider community, these men helped build the roads, the canals, the railways, the reservoirs; the ships and in WW2 the Airfields which made Britain's survival possible. Their names are on every memorial stone in the land.

In the 60s five Irish born police officers worked the town and most of the others had Scottish or Irish forbears. Two of the town's four police women were Irish.

Looking down from the hills surrounding the town and the valley in which it nestled was an awesome sight. It seemed the mill chimneys were innumerable, stretching into the distant haze at Ingrow. Only on Sunday were the mill sirens silent and the smoke reduced to a whisper as the ashes were cleared out to make way for another working week. There was quietness about Sundays which we all liked.

The Worth valley really was a beautiful place for those with eyes to see. Parkwood in any season was magnificent but in autumn it was glorious with its splendour of colour from the variety of trees growing there on a piece of land gifted to the town by the Duke of Devonshire. Cliff Castle is truly a spectacular place but for natural wildness and simplicity Parkwood has the edge viewed best from Cavendish Street or better still from above the old quarry among its leafy canopy. Up until 1914 my grandfather and his brother Fred kept their bees in the garden of Nancy's cottage in Parkwood, the last thatched cottage in Keighley.

The wooded hillside of Riddlesden with its tumbling trout streams (now sterile) was alive with birds before the Protection of Birds Act, 1954. Yellow hammers, linnets, wheatears, , woodlarks, and countless others and up on the marginal moorland areas pewits, curlews, partridges, grouse and golden plover abounded.

Arthur Scott was the gamekeeper at the Rough Howden end of the hillside. His father had been the head keeper on St. Ives estate above Long Lea. John Metcalfe, the moorland keeper at Bradup originated from Middlesmoor. They were both first class keepers and naturalists and friends of mine.

Riddlesden was my playground for I was born there and apart from a period living in Scotland during the war it was where I grew up, roaming the hills as described, tickling trout in Marley beck, rabbiting, netting hares, ferreting, bird nesting, mushrooming, bilberying, helping on the farms with haymaking, hand milking and muck spreading, getting caught with a grammar school pal picking snowdrops at East Riddlesden Hall, a place we considered our own for we were very territorial like the Worth Villagers across the river.

By the age of twelve I could shoot and had access to a shotgun which brought many a good meal home for the pot. School was not really for me and whenever possible I found an excuse to be roaming the hills as a hunter gatherer. With my finds I was occasionally encouraged to speak to the class about fossils and Neolithic flints I had found on Rivock or Ghyll Grange or on the magpies, jackdaws or jays I kept as pets at different times.

From the earliest age I knew I wanted to be a gamekeeper so I left home at fifteen to work for the aristocracy on a shooting estate near Oxford and that was where my real education began. The head keeper and his wife were both well educated, she at Cambridge so I had a good tutor who quickly rounded off some of my rough edges in manners and speech. Homesickness can be a bit of a nuisance and I was particularly smitten with that when I heard of the mill fire on Aireworth Road where seven women died. I knew one of them and my own mother had worked there in the past. As a learner keeper I earned very little but I sent what I could for the fund advertised in the Keighley News.

For my generation there was always the knowledge that National Service in the military would be due when we reached eighteen years. This had never troubled me and from a very early age I knew I would serve in a Scottish regiment as others of my family had. I was learning the highland bagpipes and chose to join the Gordon Highlanders, a regiment with a strong piping tradition. Two Pickles' had been killed in that regiment in WW2, both in their twenties, one at Anzio the other in the Reichewald. At 17 I began my training in Aberdeen.

From a solitary existence I was now part of a team training to fight terrorism. Then the Suez war blew up which disrupted everything. The battalion was in Cyprus and it was discovered I was too young to join them being the youngest member of my squad so I was chosen by the Regimental Sergeant Major to serve in the regimental police until I was 18.

It was a useful experience being in charge of some very tough prisoners, some from the Argyll's, mostly locked up for fighting, yet I got on with them and my two fellow policemen who had served in Cyprus during the emergency, one suffering injury during a forest fire. The Gordons lost 16 men during that period and altogether the army lost over 400 soldiers and over 20 police officers who had been seconded from Britain.

I was a marksman with the Lee Enfield rifle and useful with the Bren gun. Hand grenades were a problem for I was not a cricketer and couldn't 'lob' them as regulations required. So if no one was looking I threw them as I would a stone and hit the target every time.

On joining the battalion I served in Headquarters Company. During this period I continued with my piping and education, reading and learning all I could to make up for the 'half wild' years at Riddlesden. I then served in Germany and asked to be placed in a rifle company to understand how the 'real' soldiers fared!

With A Company I continued to learn about people, politics, survival skills and how we would react should the Russians choose to cross the nearby border or Iron Curtain between the Soviets and West Germany.

On those patrols we lived out of tins from Compo rations, some left-overs from WW2 and longed for fresh food. I was able to provide some of that with the aid of my rifle Major Duncan, the company commander was heard to say to the other officers, "If ever we go to war we must make sure we have Pickles with us and we'll never be short of venison and game." Some soldiers are remembered for less than that! After demob I worked for a time on a Royal estate in the highlands with the red deer. I was in my element in some of the wildest country in Britain with first class piping instructors to hand from the 51st Highland Division.

Now married I could not think of returning to the army so I took a game keeping job for a time on an estate in Kent but it was too remote. We returned North and the idea of the police seemed to satisfy my desire to 'serve the people' rather than wealthy individuals which I had tried. Perhaps my radical family background was seeping through or perhaps it was just maturity!

Before joining the police I felt the need to get a taste of industry so for a short time I worked in a mill office in Keighley then a factory office in the same town. The experience I gained there was invaluable and I made some lasting friends. I was accepted into the West Riding Constabulary in 1961 and trained near Harrogate. The ex-Scots Guards drill instructor selected me as class leader on account of my Infantry training and knowledge of drill. The class was mostly ex-servicemen with a few ex-police cadets. I passed out second from the top of the class and was posted to Keighley, a town with the highest crime rate in the County and there I learned some valuable lessons and a little more humility!

My pal and I on regimental duty; a change from our usual Bren gun team but as 19 year olds, all good practice for the West Riding.

Chapter 2

The Big Lesson

I stood motionless in the recess of the old carpet shop doorway from which I could survey the whole of Keighley town's ancient covered market. It had rained hard during the whole of my shift on number 4 beat and I was cold and wet through despite the protection of the Melton cape which reached only to my knees. Outside on the pavement the drains were overflowing and large rats ran from those without covers, squealing; scurrying to safety among the leftovers from the wooden stalls. What a dump it was. The whole town was now a dump with massive demolition and cheap, shoddy reconstruction but this was 1961, a time for change!

The rain continued to lash down and more rats went scampering by.

A drunken couple lurched into the market. By the street light I saw it was a lady of the night with her client. As she was about to earn her fee over the counter of the fruit and veg stall I coughed quietly but deeply enough for the couple to hear. They departed hurriedly. In another quarter of an hour it would be time to go off duty nor would I be sorry for I was truly frozen to the marrow.

When quietly watching and waiting for something to happen the brain was ever active for there was so much to learn and those periods of quietness were never wasted. The relevance of learning law preoccupied much of my time for the law was now my stock in trade!

It was then I noticed a shadowy figure sidling down between the stalls towards the lock-up butchers shop. By the light of the gas lamp I saw it was a man about my age of twenty-two. The next moment the chap was throwing himself at the shop door, trying to break in using bodily pressure.

Any old-time bobby would have allowed the man to break in then he would have arrested him on the premises or when leaving with the loot. For me this was a dilemma. With only ten minutes to go before the end of my tour I knew if I made an arrest I would be up all night preparing a case for court in the morning. Was it not true that a constable's first duty was to prevent crime? With that I sprang into action, running the short distance to the shop door and grabbing hold of the miscreant before he could do any damage. He did not resist.

The poor fellow was soaked to the skin, utterly dejected and very frightened. I discovered he was living rough, out of work and starving which was why he had sought food at the butchers, hoping for a left-over meat pie. He told me had been in a road accident receiving severe head injuries. I had to think quickly or I would be missed at roll-call in the station.

My beliefs persuaded me to let the man go. He didn't need a ticking off or a caution; he knew he was in the wrong. He was desperate and in need of help. In the next street was a fish and chip shop so we walked through the torrent to the steamy, warmth of the shop and I paid for his supper. Before leaving I arranged to meet him on the library steps at 10 a.m. next day. It is right and proper to help another soul in distress but I confess to feeling a little uneasy about this one.

The morning after was my rest day. I was at the library as promised when the unfortunate man mounted the steps. I gave him a chitty, written permission to be supplied with a hot meal at a certain local café. The man was grateful but said little being in a depressed and hopeless state. Social Services were in their infancy or did not exist at all so there was nowhere but the workhouse to send him and he would not agree to that. We parted on the steps and I got on with my rest day – a long walk on the Leeds and Liverpool canal.

The canal walk was nearly over but now I passed the place where I had seen my first dead body just after the war at the age of eleven. It was a man, fully clothed, lying on the towpath. A policeman was already present so I did not go too close. My job was to gather as many acorns as I could carry to feed the pigs for they loved them and we loved the pigs, even though we eventually ate them. I had grown up with animals and was familiar with living and dead things. It was all perfectly natural though I was sad for the unknown victim of drowning in the 'cut' our name for the canal. One of my family also drowned in the canal; another, just a boy, drowned in the river Aire.

The following morning I got up early and went for a run. I felt the need to keep fit as it was obvious to me that many police officers were not physically fit. I had expected gymnasiums in every division such as every barracks had. There were none and it was left to each individual to keep fit in his own way.

On my way back I passed the newsagents and saw the bill-board. It said "Man wanted for murder". I knew instinctively who it was and that I had made a terrible mistake by being lenient with the man in the market.

When going on duty we paraded a quarter of an hour before our shift started but were never paid for that. By a quarter to two I knew for certain the man being sought was the man I had helped. What could I do? What should I do? After his brief court appearance it was my luck to be detailed to take the prisoner to jail at Armley.

We both sat in the back of the transit van in silence, he with his head down, me wishing I could have put the clock back. "You should have arrested me in the market," was all he said. "Yes, I should have done," I replied. It was an awkward journey and neither of us said another word.

The fellow had got into a fight and killed his opponent then set fire to the derelict property they were squatting in. He was sent to prison but after his release he killed a woman. The arresting officer at the time never commented to me even if he knew of the part I had played in giving him chits for food at the café.

The moral to the tale is that the enforcement of the law must come before selfish considerations or the welfare of the offender but I was learning! Neither could I have foreseen the consequences but it did trouble me, more so, years later when I learned of the second death; the subsequent saving of lives during my service tended to balance things out for even they were the result of pure chance and being there at the right time.

Addingham's derelict Police house and Office just prior to demolition.

Chapter 3

The Cyclist

I was on night duty and the rain was torrential. Standing unobserved in a junk-shop doorway, a venue for much stolen property, I moved from one foot to the other to keep warm. There was not much traffic up the Halifax Road but it was already half-past midnight and the pubs were long closed.

From the direction of the town cross came a strange sound; a rhythmic, metallic sound. Looking to my right I could see a cyclist approaching slowly, weaving from one side of the road to the other, his head down, singing to himself. The sound came from his unlit machine as he drunkenly urged his ancient steed forward at great risk to life and limb.

It was like something out of a comical film especially when he turned right and tried to cycle up the gable end of a terrace house wall. At that point I intervened for he fell heavily to the wet pavement with the cycle on top of him. His singing stopped abruptly for he was winded.

"Come on, old chap," said I helping him to his feet, "I'll walk you home." For what good it did I might as well have spoken to the wall. He was quite incoherent; not a word could I understand. As luck would have it there was a blue painted police pillar nearby from which I summoned transport. With difficulty we rolled him into the back of the car to be taken to the police station while I followed on pushing his bike.

Two officers were still trying to extricate him from the police car on my arrival for he had fallen fast asleep. Placed safely in a cell he returned to that land of dreams.

His name was Sean Smith and his home was so near where I had found him. He appeared in the Magistrates court that morning when he pleaded guilty and was fined £8. Sean was one of thousands of Irish descent who had come to the town following the potato famine or farm evictions from Connaught but more especially from counties Mayo, Sligo and Leitrim. Many had married into their own Catholic compatriots whilst others, like mine, had married into local Yorkshire stock from Haworth.

At first my father was not pleased with me for arresting one of his fisherman friends but finally accepted it was for his own safety, recalling a wager Mr Smith had undertaken to eat a raw, full-sized trout whilst drinking at the Black Horse in Low Street. Apparently he did it too but was promptly very sick and all for ten shillings. Strong drink certainly lands men in trouble!

Some months later Mr Smith did a most silly thing after a drinking spell. He was trying to light his fire and failing. On the floor of the cellar–head he kept two identical cans; one full of paraffin, the other full of petrol. A drop of paraffin sometimes got him out of his dilemma when the wind was wrong in the chimney and there was little danger from it. I never did learn why he kept a can of petrol but that night it nearly did for him. Choosing the wrong can he poured petrol over the smouldering heap of sticks and coal. In an instant the petrol exploded setting Sean alight and badly burning him. He was a long time recovering but those descendants of Ballina, Bunnyconolon and Kilgarvan in Mayo were made of tough stuff. I last saw him singing Yeats song the 'Sally Gardens' on a sunny day in the Town Hall Square, still content with his lot as he waited for the bus to go fishing. As for the cycling incident he never bore me a grudge, nor did he ever learn who had paid his fine!

There were many like Sean, originally from Irish farming stock exiled into this dark, satanic mill town. But for the famine, the evictions, the civil war his kind would have been tilling the soil, tending their sheep and cows and happily bringing up their families, speaking their native Gaelic language and enjoying religious freedom in the magnificent countryside that had been their home since time began.

Speaking of the Gaels reminds me of the time I had to see the manager of Hattersley's Mill off South Street. There had been some on-going damage to cars parked outside the Spiritualist church near the mill. As fate would have it `I detected the culprit and brought the matter to an end.

Talking to the manager about the looms the firm made for the Harris Tweed Industry he assured me they still carried on that trade. I had served with men from those two islands of Harris and Lewis and knew some of those looms were very ancient but still serviceable. Producing a letter from his filing cabinet he shewed me one recently sent from Lewis for a spare part for a loom. The crofter stated the loom had been bought by his grandfather from Keighley in the 1840s but had developed a fault in the weaving and asked if a spare part could be sent. The manager assured me it was. Perhaps the looms were made too well to last over a hundred years but that was the way of British Manufacturing and perhaps the cause of their demise.

On being required to give a talk to a class of young children at Parkwood School during the tenure of head teacher Mr. Colin Hudson, I tried to concentrate on the natural history to be found in the valley and the Neolithic evidence of our ancestors with the flint arrowheads and scrapers I had found. When I had finished the talk I asked if there were any questions. A number put up their hands but one little lad at the front was nearly bursting to ask his question which was:

"Sir, Sir, where did you get that scar on your forehead?"

I didn't tell him it was partly from a fight with an older boy and my tripping over a mat in the gym when playing pirates and colliding head-on with a radiator. I told him the latter for both were true. To notice the unusual is a good quality in a police officer. Perhaps this boy had the gift!

Children will always get up to mischief in snow throwing snowballs and when one boy threw one at a window of a dentist's surgery up Devonshire Street it could have had serious consequences. The window broke and the snow and glass splinters showered all over the patient and the dentist. Fortunately the youth was caught and dealt with.

Mischief Night, the eve of plot night, was a dangerous time for those taking part in the age-old tradition and the intended victims. One young boy placed a firework on the step of a council house, lit the banger, knocked on the door and ran away. A heavily pregnant lady answered the door just as the firework went off. She subsequently lost the baby. The young boy was dealt with but his parents were not cooperative which did not work in his interest. At the time we did not know she would lose the baby and the boy would likely have been cautioned for his stupid but forgivable childish behaviour. The hostility of some parents towards the Police when one of their offspring was accused was a great sadness for it often led to a parent being prosecuted for a breach of the peace or worse and jeopardised any common-sense solution to the problem but as they say, 'there's now't na queerer than folk!'

The police bent over backwards to avoid prosecuting juveniles, for once they had the stigma of a criminal conviction it could mark them for the rest of their lives, cast doubt on their suitability for employment or higher education. Children will always push the bounds; that is how they learn. With more serious criminal offences such as burglary, break ins and stealing the juvenile court usually followed but it was an improvement of the previous century when they might have been sent to Botany Bay!

Chapter 4

The First Post Mortem

Most post mortems are quickly forgotten or merge into one but this was my first. When a sudden death was reported the officer working that beat automatically became Coroner's Officer and dealt with it. Like many others I was thrown in at the deep end and this one demanded a great deal of tact and diplomacy for the deceased was a nun who had been staying at a retreat for nuns when she died.

I knocked gently on the door and was admitted by a nun clearly in authority but kindly and eager to help the police. The death of the sister was unexpected; she had not been ill nor had she been seen by a doctor within fourteen days. Had that been the case a death certificate might have been issued and the police and Coroner would not have been involved. The Mother Superior understood that and could throw no light on the death other than the sister had retired to bed after communal prayers.

I was led into the room where she was lying, her face uncovered, serene, at peace with a hint of a smile about her lips. Someone had placed her arms across her chest. I explained the undertaker would have to remove the body to the mortuary at the Victoria Hospital; she nodded that she understood.

Victoria Hospital had seen better days and was due for demolition like most other interesting buildings in town. The mortuary was round the back, part of the Pathology Department and it was to this we conveyed the deceased with as much reverence as we could.

Thinking of post-mortem examinations conjured up all manner of thoughts. Obviously there had to be an external examination to check for any injuries which might have contributed to death but beyond that, in my simple countryman case, I believed that to be enough.

Seeing the poor soul uncovered on the slab and the doctor making that first incision even today seemed an unacceptable violation of a human being, sacrilegious even in view of the person we were dealing with. However, the doctor taught me much that day. His death report showed the lady had died of heart failure, a common cause of death locally.

Being present at the whole of this examination my eyes wandered round the old building. It would not have passed muster in the former SS barracks I had last occupied where cleanliness was a fanatical obsession not only with the Germans who had built the place aided by Jewish forced labour in 1939, the year I was born in this same hospital.

I came off duty early that day to find my wife had made an excellent dinner of steak and kidney pie. I pushed it away and told her I could not eat it. She was not pleased. I tried to explain without going into too much detail but for the moment at least I was off such food. I did not know it at the time but I had picked up a bug in the mortuary.

The following day the doctor was sent for and he diagnosed gastro-enteritis. I had severe stomach pains, was constantly sick and felt as though I would die. A single bed was erected downstairs and there I lay for two weeks, the doctor visiting daily. I lost considerable weight and indeed looked like death, in my striped pyjamas, not unlike the poor inmates of Belsen Concentration camp which I had visited in the 50s. Gradually I recovered from the bug but in a way I was glad the old Victorian Hospital was pulled down and burned. How else can years of infection be destroyed but by fire. At my next post-mortem I told the pathologist Dr Stewart of my illness after my previous visit but he was dismissive. I said nothing. Well, I'm told even the police have been known to close ranks when faced with adverse criticism!

Post mortems were to be endured for they were part of our duty but there were pleasanter things to be doing. The first one was perhaps easier for me being used to dealing with deer carcases in the highlands; hoisting a stag up on a block and tackle and skinning it with the sharpest of knives or skinning a sheep to feed the dogs in similar fashion or burning the hairs off a large pig in a pile of straw before dissecting it to find the cause of death before that too was boiled up and fed to the dogs. All this was part of country life, something I and my forebears had always accepted. The catching of rabbits and hares was a seasonal thing like plucking pheasants, grouse, partridges, ducks or geese. Like post mortems we just got on with it though I was never the 'pheasant plucker's son'!

Dr Bates showed me the difference between a smoker's lungs and those of a non-smoker. A non-smoker had pink healthy lungs whereas with the heavy smoker they were like Gorgonzola cheese, black and horrible. I sometimes wished smokers could attend and see the harm they were inflicting on themselves!

The most dreadful mortuary I ever encountered was the one in Silsden, just off Howden Road. If Victoria Hospital mortuary was of that era the Silsden mortuary was medieval, though it did have electricity and the wooden blocks to place beneath the heads of the cadavers were of solid elm! No one wants such a place to get too warm but in winter it was freezing and even the saws and other operating tools rusted over.

Its worst aspect was when the examination was over and the body sewn up and washed down. The drain out in the street would overflow with blood, hair, bone and worse, running down the street. The duty constable did his best as I oft had done but it was a public disgrace and one didn't have to be a doctor to realise the health risk. Complaints brought temporary relief but it wasn't until the hospital at Airedale was operational that the place was closed for good and converted into a house!

Officers were used to clearing up blood and gore at the scene of road accidents but to see sergeant Abbott supervising a P.C. swilling the blood off the road outside a public building was not edifying! There was enough of that at road accident scenes.

Dr John Bates was one of the pathologist team who would kindly explain what he was doing and why, welcoming any questions. He was a Major with the Territorial Army and one day told me he would not 'make old bones'! I suppose when one is involved in such work one recognised the symptoms.

On one occasion after numerous post mortems where the cause of death was fairly apparent from the patient's life style and environment I asked him out of all he had carried out, how many were there that he could not have honestly foreseen? Two, he said, the rest was routine!

The opening of Airedale Hospital by my then Colonel in Chief The Prince of Wales whom I guarded that day along with one or two others brought much improvement in the pathology department with Drs Tinsley and Pirrah in charge and eventually leading to a permanent Coroner's Officer in Sergeant Les Allison one time Riddlesden Bobbie and former Keighley C.I.D.

Oak tree living at Bolton Abbey when the Normans first came with their office of Constable.

Chapter 5

Vic in Charge

Vic was an old soldier with two strands of medal ribbons on his chest. He had never taken promotion but was frequently asked to be in charge of a shift if a sergeant was absent. A rough, gruff man of few words and then, often scathing about someone or other. He was not very smart, often arriving for the early morning shift covered in dandruff with shaving cream still on his face but for all that he was a shrewd judge of character and a good policeman. His accent was of South Yorkshire, rarely was he without a cigarette and one could imagine him off duty spending his time propping up the bar with a pint of Timothy Taylors a man to whom he was very respectful when he was chairman of the Magistrates before he went to the House of Lords.

If there was a full complement of sergeants Vic would be responsible for the 999 car which permitted him to spend more time in the station keeping warm and reading Police Reports which we were all supposed to read. Only once did I see anything useful and that was a photograph of a soldier of my own regiment who I had served with in the 50s. He was a bad lot then and clearly had not improved.

The last words to Vic, before he settled with a cup of tea in the mess room, were to fill up the Austin Westminster car with petrol. More concerned with the football results and his Littlewood coupons, Vic forgot. It could have had serious consequences for the old car had problems and was never entirely reliable on starting. It was a common sight seeing two or three burly Bobbies pushing her off. Such an indignity thought some of the Aldermen! What was the police force coming to?

Saturday nights were always busy. Some officers prayed for rain knowing a good shower was worth ten constables. The whole shift was tied up when a 999 call came in that a car had been stolen and was being driven off towards Skipton. Vic came to life, jumped in the Westminster alone and started her up. It was one of those rare occasions when she responded. Soon he was travelling along the trunk road passed the town cemetery. Once outside the speed limit he accelerated and caught up with the stolen car. It increased speed taking advantage of the blind bends for the thief knew how to drive.

The Westminster started to cough and Vic remembered he had not filled up with petrol as ordered. He cursed under his breath and made one desperate effort to catch the stolen car as it entered a sharp left-hand bend by Hawcliffe Tower. The Westminster cruised to a standstill with an empty tank and Vic thought he had seen the last of his quarry. He sat fuming at the wheel trying to radio for assistance when he heard the sound of a collision beyond the bend. Completing his message, he left the police car where she had stalled, walked quickly round the bend to find the criminal trapped in the car but not seriously injured.

Vic knew the miscreant by name. He was responsible for stealing numerous cars. The Magistrates didn't know what to do with him. Vic knew he would eventually cause someone's death and go down for a long time. Did they really have to wait for that to happen? Sergeant Haigh congratulated Vic on his success but he knew only half of the story.

There is a long-lasting memory of this likeable P.C. when dismissing the shift for their tour of duty: "Right, pick up your parrots and monkeys and fall in facing the boat!"

There had been a heavy fall of snow and it was freezing cold. We were all wearing pyjamas beneath our thick serge trousers, a greatcoat and a cape. Working number one beat I knew I was considered to be trusted by Sergeant Robinson who set up the duty roster. This trust was not easily given and even then grudgingly or that was how it seemed. This beat contained all the banks, prestigious properties and all that seemed to matter including the Town Hall.

Standing near to the police pillar at the junction making my point, an appointment we made every hour at a given time I saw the 999 car approaching. This time Vic was driving the Morris Oxford, another clapped out old banger. Sergeant Haigh was in the passenger seat. All Vic said was "Get in" in his usual uncouth way. We drove in silence to the top of the town and up the steep hill towards the hospital area. I feared another sudden death so I deigned to ask what was going on. Vic said nothing but Sergeant Haigh, another war veteran with double medal ribbons explained.

"You know we've been having a lot of burglaries on number two beat well a woman has just rung in saying she's seen a man answering the description going from house to house. He's wearing a black beret, carrying a brief case and pushing a bicycle."

Tom was the best sergeant anyone could have. A family man with sons of his own who would later join the police. He served with distinction in the army but said little about it. I know when it ended he was practically running his battalion and the only way he got demobbed was to trick his colonel into signing his discharge papers for he did not wish to lose him. Returning to the police he had attended the detective training school and was well versed in law but somewhere along the line he had upset someone and was still a sergeant. It did not seem to trouble him for he had a great sense of humour and to those who were prepared to listen passed on his knowledge which helped during quiet night patrols.

"There he is," said Vic, driving the car through the deep slushy snow to stop an inch from the suspect and his bicycle. "Get his bike," was all he said to me.

Still at the wheel with the window down he growled at the suspect "Get in!"

The man protested, "But, but, but!" he said.

Vic shouted the order more forcibly, "Get in!" The chap got in and off the three of them drove leaving me with the bike. I pushed it all the way downhill because of the icy conditions which took a little time. At least I was a lot warmer!

In the parade room there stood a long trestle table. It was covered in piles of money of all denominations: pound notes, ten shilling notes, silver and copper. The sergeant stood opposite me as I entered. He wore a wry grin and as our eyes met he lifted his to the ceiling stifling a chuckle. Vic stood at the end of the table addressing the man they had brought in. He was ringing his hands like a money lender his face bearing a fake, embarrassed smile.

"Well you see Sir," he said, "These things happen from time to time in our job. No harm's done, is it and you won't want to make a complaint, will you?"

I'd seen men eat humble pie before; tasted it myself but this show by Vic was the best performance ever. They shook hands and gathered the money back into the case and I returned the poor chap's bike. As he started back up the hill he was visibly shaking with fear but he never did complain. Now, had he been the villain it would have been a different story instead of a hapless rent collector going about his lawful business but that was Vic!

Less abruptness, a few questions at the scene perhaps could have prevented the mistake. It was all good learning material and something very embarrassing to avoid in the future!

Chapter 6

No Smoke without Fire

With the approach of the Christmas season the geese may have been getting fat. Certainly the town's thieves were. Mainly it was the numerous working men's clubs that were the night-time targets, cigarettes and spirits being the prize. Two of us were put on plain-clothes duty to concentrate on the premises likely to be on the list of attack. We worked alone carrying torch, staff and handcuffs. It was different; a change but we still had to ring in each hour and from our parting at the station I would not likely see my colleague until the shift was over at 6 a.m.

We were still having real winters, starting in November and carrying on, sometimes until Whitsuntide. Snowfalls were often heavy and frosts very severe. There was a severe frost this night. Our footwear was rubber soled boots which made no noise but we still carried our chrome whistle just in case though I had never used it yet.

The thieves were very ingenious in gaining entry to premises by choosing sites we would not easily notice for instance climbing up a wall or drainpipe and breaking a window out of view. Cellar-heads were another likely spot, where the barrels were lowered down but sometimes, when they had had a few they just broke the door down and took their chance.

Night patrols of this nature for the non-inquisitive officer could have been tedious but for those with half a brain it was an opportunity to study law with a view to becoming a better bobby or just to learn about the stars and the night sky, all of great interest.

The night settled down to near silence. Few cars moved after midnight and those that did were likely to be stopped and the occupants checked out. It was all about crime prevention and detection and it worked. It was amazing what turned up on those routine spot-checks. In fact, no one could put a price on the value of a patrolling constable, whether he was just standing at the pavement edge watching people coming and going, seeing children or old people across the road or standing like a choreographed marionette in the middle of the street doing traffic duty at busy times. His presence alone was enough to deter many from lawlessness and he certainly reassured the righteous and decent section of the community.

The Warp Dressers and Twisters club was secure but a noise round the back drew my attention. Shining my torch I got a glimpse of a young couple copulating against the wall. The light was on them for barely a second for I did not wish them to be disturbed. Anyone as keen as them on such a cold night deserved their pleasure for it truly was brass monkey weather.

The parish church clock struck one. Another hour and I would be allowed back at the station for a three quarter of an hour break with a cup of tea and a sandwich my wife had packed. I could only eat jam sandwiches on night duty which drew some amusement and was very different from Patrick or Vic's cooking bacon and eggs on the dirty old stove, smelling the place out like a transport café.

My colleague Patrick had taken his break at 1.a.m.and was now out on the prowl again. It was good to be in the warmth of the mess-room for a short time, to listen to the banter and watch the others playing cards. Every one of us had been in the forces, either National Service or in WW2. Each had a story to tell. On such a night it was good to hear Vic describe one of his fellow constables' experiences during the war. It was the cards that reminded him. His pal had been in the Royal Flying Corps during WW1 then joined the police force. There was an airfield on his rural beat and he took his break there having a cup of tea with the mixed bag of officers and sergeants and sometimes joined in the card game they played whilst waiting to go on a raid. They knew he was one of them from the previous war and sometimes tempted him with the offer of a flight with them over enemy territory which he always declined. Tonight, however, he had heard of a good friend being killed in Tunisia, had imbibed in a couple of pints to try and raise his spirits. These airmen knew nothing of his loss and this time when they asked him if he'd like to come with them he agreed. Their destination was Essen. The bombs were loaded and the planes waiting on the tarmac.

At the appointed time the constable boarded the Lancaster being assured by the pilot they would get him back safely in time for him to report going off duty. According to Vic they did get him back and it did do something for morale. I was assured the tale was true. All I could think of if they had been shot down and this West Riding constable floating down on his parachute in his cape and helmet and the expression on the faces of his captors and what would Hitler have thought of it. He might have had him shot as a fifth columnist.

I was out again and the first club I checked I sensed something was wrong. A ground floor window was just ajar with some empty crates stacked beneath it. I listened and sure enough there was a sound from within. There was a telephone kiosk just fifty yards away. My message for assistance took only a moment. I then returned to keep observations, feeling the comfort of my staff against my right thigh.

Out of my eye corner I saw a road traffic patrol car silently roll up near the gate without lights. It was Walter, a grand reliable, son of a gamekeeper from up the Dales. Sergeant Haigh was with him. With one of us on three sides of the building we had a good chance of catching the intruder where ever he broke cover. Like a hare he came out where he'd gone in, straight into the arms of gentle Walter who promptly gave him a gentle smack at the side of his head warning him not to do anything stupid.

When the key holder came we found two boxes of spirits stacked ready for removal. The fellow lived nearby and it transpired he was working alone but was out of work and hard up, a poor excuse for dishonesty. Walter and the sergeant dealt with the arrest and I carried on with my club checks.

By five thirty I was getting tired and headed back towards the town centre checking the less likely places of attack. Looking across the derelict waste where only recently a fine church had stood I crossed the pinfold (where livestock was once impounded) which became the Irish quarter in Queen Victoria's reign.

Due to the heavy, white frost, steam was emanating from various openings in the roofs and walls of various properties but there was one building where it did not seem right. Beyond the waste area were old back to back cottages so common in the town. Steam seemed to be coming from its chimney and all its ventilation holes but was it steam or smoke. I hurried across. There was not a soul about and it was smoke alright; I could smell it. The house was on fire.

The curtains were drawn downstairs and smoke was coming through the letter box and gaps in the door. The bedroom curtains were also drawn. The only escape route was through the door and unless the people were already overcome by smoke they would still be sleeping. I also knew from past experience that as soon as that door opened the room would likely burst into flame.

Banging hard on the door with my staff I was relieved to see two frightened faces at the bedroom window. I shouted for them to cover their mouths and make quickly for the house door. There I waited anxiously. It seemed an age but it was only seconds before I heard them at the door and then they were out into the street and the room erupted in flames as I slammed the door shut again.

The banging and shouting had awoken neighbours and they took the couple in. I sent a passer-by to ring for the fire brigade and an ambulance to check the couple for smoke inhalation and then I walked quickly and quietly away from the scene of the little drama. I needed to be back at the station for six otherwise they would be searching for me.

No one at the scene knew I was a police officer and why should they need to. It was pure chance me being there at the right time and I am glad I was. No one at the station knew and I never told anyone. I had done what I was expected to do – save life. It had a better feeling than perhaps causing the loss of life. With longer service I found that the two had a habit of balancing out each other not unlike a G.P. or a surgeon. Sort of win some lose some but at least this policing had variety!

Beamsley Beacon from Addingham.
Photograph courtesy of John Milner of Addingham Moorside.

Chapter 7

Christmas Eve

We stood at ease in the parade room as the shift always did at the start of our tour of duty. Sergeant Haigh read from the clip-board the crimes and incidents we needed to know about. He then brought us to attention and gave the order 'appointments'. As a drill movement each constable produced his staff in his right hand and his hand-cuffs in his left." Tonight we want no prisoners," he said, "Unless it is unavoidable; Good will towards men and a Happy Christmas to you all. To your duties dismiss."

The town was busy; there was a feeling of excitement in the air; the streets were illuminated; in the square opposite the police station a huge Christmas tree stood dwarfing the statues of the soldier and sailor figures on the war memorial. Carols were being sung by a mixed church choir and it was just lovely.

I was glad to be on number one beat for that was where most of the people were and tonight was special. Local historian and librarian Ian Dewhurst was beaming as he passed me on the library steps, always a good view point. The colour in his cheeks was not just the cold, I thought as other staff exited the building full of good cheer with perhaps a drop of something from Walls Rum!

Slowly patrolling North Street I passed Freddie and his brother, both meth drinkers well known to everyone, especially the police. Freddie gave me a sly grin. Stony-faced I walked down Low Street where I was amazed to see how busy Mosely's fish and chip restaurant was as were others in High Street and Temple Row. Perhaps some people would not be having a turkey dinner tomorrow.

Just after midnight I was joined by the Sergeant. We passed a number of people worse for drink or just merry depending on your point of view but all was good humoured and friendly. One very jolly chap came up close offering us a share of his fish and chips. In a slurred voice with a grin from ear to ear he tempted the two of us. "Come on officer, have a chip." We declined but he was having none of that. "Officer, I'm offering you one of my chips. Why do you refuse? They're good chips. Was that a hint of belligerence I wondered; we didn't want a fracas so to please him we each took a chip from his newspaper wrapped bundle. That pleased him. His grin widened. "Salt of the earth," he said nodding to a passer-by. "Where would we be without the boys in blue," he added. "Goodnight officers God Bless and Merry Christmas."

When some distance away the sergeant told me the man had been a famous prize boxer until he suffered brain damage." He was intelligent too; a sergeant-major in the Paras; got the Military Medal at Arnhem. You don't get that for nothing."

We walked along in silence for a while.

"Did you box?" asked the sergeant.

"We had to," I replied, "Dargai Day; a battle the Gordons took part in on the North West Frontier where one of our pipers got the Victoria Cross for playing with both legs shot through and another piper the Distinguished Conduct Medal. This event was celebrated with sport including boxing every year."

"Were you any good?" asked the sergeant.

"Well I knocked out two of my opponents from 'B' Company but then had to fight a Geordie lad from 'A' Company, my own company. He was semi-professional; talk about seeing stars; he half killed me. He left to join the SAS soon after. I think he would have done well there but he cured me of boxing!"

The sergeant laughed. "Self-inflicted wounds never made any sense to me. I've seen so many with permanent brain damage I am amazed there isn't a law against it but it's about gambling and as long as there's money to be made young men will be lured into it. If only they knew what it could lead to."

There was a commotion from Hanover Street. It was just three well-oiled drunken men having a laugh.

"What time is the last bus?" asked one of them.

"You're from Parkwood and there's no bus now so get a taxi."

"Can you get us one officer, we've got money, and we can pay for it."

The Taxi rank was just round the corner so I did as they asked.

They were all big heavyweights and bordering on being incapable but we wanted no prisoners tonight.

We pushed, pulled and shoved two of them into the vehicle with much fun and banter when I took hold of the last reveller by his right arm, propelling him through the door. He got stuck so I applied a bit more force. A sickly feeling permeated to the pit of my stomach. What had I done? His right arm sleeve had gone slack in my hand. There had been the sound of a crack and then it was empty. Crazy thoughts went through my mind. Had I broken it; was he suffering from some mysterious illness. He suddenly burst out laughing, crawled onto the seat and sat up. His pals too were laughing their heads off. One of them reached down to the taxi floor and lifted up an artificial arm. The relief I felt at that moment cannot be expressed. Seconds before I had seen my police career ended; now it was my turn to laugh.

"You should have seen your face!" said the sergeant, "I'll bet you never forget that little incident.

The taxi drove away at last. "Come on," said the sergeant, "It's time we did some proper policing."

"There's Freddie the meth drinker," said the sergeant.

"What on earth is he up to?" said I.

"I know what the blighter's up to," said the sergeant, "He's after getting his Christmas dinner. Quick, try and catch him."

"He's got something in his hand," I said.

"Yes he will have; it will be a building brick, come on; let's stop him."

We ran towards the man sidling up to the bank. Just before we reached him his right arm went back and the brick sailed through the bank window immediately setting off the alarm. Freddie did not run away but sat down on the pavement against the bank wall. One or two passers-by stopped to look. We stood looking down at Freddie and the sergeant wagged his finger at him.

"I've told you before. If you want a Christmas dinner go to Bradford. You'll get no Christmas dinner here." A small crowd had gathered now and with Freddie on the ground and us two giants standing over him it looked bad."

"Pick on someone your own size," said a drunken voice with a distinctive Glasgow accent.

"Are you from Maryhill," I asked the Jock.

"I am frae Maryhill," he replied in amazement, "How did yea ken that?"

"Bygone," I said, "Before I tell you more about yourself," for it was only his accent that gave him away. I'd served with many Glaswegians and was interested in dialect. The man, looking puzzled, left the scene as did the rest of them. Freddie was reluctantly arrested and placed in the cells. He thought he had achieved his objective but next day there was no roast turkey with trimmings and no Christmas pudding; just a mug of strong Yorkshire tea, a bowl of vegetable soup and a sardine sandwich. He looked disgusted but it was more than he would have got on the street and we did add an ice bun with a cherry on top. A special court on Boxing Day saw a further offence added to the long list and he was bound over to keep the peace plus costs for repair to the bank window. He was lucky not to get charged with stealing the building brick for it was a new one but we didn't know where he got it from.

Chapter 8

Accidents Will Happen

For any police officer road accidents are common place and were usually followed by a prosecution which seemed unfair for both parties had experienced shock, injury and damage and to the likes of me that seemed enough. Compulsory insurance meant those companies would have the last word and unless someone (very rare) had deliberately caused the accident, what was the point of causing more suffering?

It was midnight, pouring with rain and I was returning off my beat to discard my sodden cape and put on a waterproof coat when a car pulled up.

"There's a road accident by the cemetery," he said, "Just one car on a bad bend; no one is hurt."

I knew both 999 cars were out and no one else available to attend but me. He must have been reading my thoughts because he said, "I can take you there if it will help."

I thanked the man, nipped in the station to ask them to send a breakdown for a Ford Popular saloon and jumped in. This volunteering by the public was quite typical in those days. They were eager to help and this particular night I was glad for it was near to Utley; a steady walk otherwise.

The damaged car could not have been in a more dangerous position, right across the centre of the road in a patch of dark shadow where the street lights were not working. The driver explained how he entered the bend and aquaplaned before colliding with a cherry tree and bouncing back into the road. He had a lucky escape and would shortly have another.

The road was awash with rain water and there was no let-up in the wind which was bringing branches down off the ornamental trees on each side. Thankfully, traffic was light.

Concerned that I had only my lamp on my night belt to warn traffic I went to investigate some road works a hundred yards away. There were six paraffin lamps around them so I borrowed two. At least they were better than nothing. Placing one at each end of the obstruction I stepped back onto the pavement to join the driver. Scarcely had I done so, feeling quite pleased at my initiative when the whole of the road burst into flame, including the car. Unknown to me the road was awash with leaked petrol. I turned to the driver, "Bloody hell," he said, then kindly-like, "Don't worry lad, t'car was knackered."

I nodded foolishly and was further embarrassed when a chap came from a nearby house, "I've sent for the Fire Brigade," he said. I recognised him as special constable Haigh. It transpired he'd watched the whole incident but became useful in the end. The regular police did not strictly approve of specials.

The road was soon cleared and the driver and I walked back to the police station. Over a hot drink he joked about his loss and we both had a laugh. Well, not every probationary constable sets fire not just to the road but to a car as well. Yet another lesson was learned. The driver blamed the rain. I did not smell the petrol nor did I see it but my actions could have resulted in serious injury and I knew it.

A theft of money had occurred at a house in Worth Village and Tommy Dawson C.I.D (later MBE) and I attended. It was not a large amount of money but it mattered to the lady owner who suspected one of her visitors. In searching the suspect's handbag Tommy found a hole in the lining and lo and behold, there was the missing money pushed through. On returning to the police station Superintendent Verity happened to be there as Tommy passed by with a big grin and his prisoner. The Super liked to see his men catching thieves.

Tommy was aliens' officer at Keighley at a time when all aliens had to report to the police station each week. He chose to return to being a beat Bobby up on the border with Lancashire and it was there he was awarded the MBE for services to the community.

Crime detection mattered and not just to CID. A notice hung on the wall giving a record of crimes reported and crimes detected and woe betide us if it should become disproportionate; it was then that T.I.Cs came in useful (taken into consideration)! On being called to what appeared at first to be a road accident up Guardhouse I arrived just as the ambulance was about to leave but there was no sign of any vehicle. The ambulance man told me they had found the man lying in the road bleeding badly. As they drove off to Victoria hospital I began following the trail of blood up the road eventually to a garden gate. The householder's brother had left shortly before and was known to be very ill. He was in fact dead on arrival at the hospital for his lungs had burst.

One of the old Keighley residents told me how it used to be in Keighley before the National Health Service with whole families dying within a few days from tuberculosis.

Each day brought varied tasks from dealing with a lady dementia patient who asked me to walk her home and accepting what she told me was correct only to find after a considerable distance that her home had been demolished twenty years before. She was a very convincing poor soul but we persevered and found out where she really belonged. There was quite a lot of this.

Another disturbed lady took me to the ruins of dam side where she was convinced she had laid her dead baby, pointing the very spot in the remains of a house where I was obliged to scratch about in the soil. Finding nothing I walked her back home where her husband explained she was not taking her medication and that the story of the baby was in her mind. He agreed to get her doctor.

An indecent exposure to school children in Victoria Park led to the man being caught by the park attendant and me interviewing him. He did not deny the offence and pleaded guilty in court. This sort of thing tended to happen in hot weather.

One tweed clad middle-aged lady golfer on the Keighley course at Utley complained of a man exposing himself to her from across the river as she was about to tee off. When I interviewed her she gave a perfect description and on being asked the delicate question as to whether the man might have been spending a penny she was adamant he was not; the next question was whether he was 'excited' " Oh yes very much so," she said with confidence.

"But madam," I said gently, "You say you were on the 2nd hole which is a long way from the river where the man was standing."

"Ah yes, officer, but you see, I had these with me," and reached inside her pocket and pulled out a pair of 8X30 binoculars. "I find them very useful for bird watching," she said.

She must have frightened him up to Branshaw Golf Club for there was no other complaint from the Keighley course.

About this time an unusually sad incident occurred when P.C. Robin Dadswell was detailed to deal with a sudden death which had occurred in South Africa. Because the body was placed in a sealed metal casket and had been delivered into our Police District for burial the Coroner was involved. Great difficulty was experienced cutting through the metal of the casket and P.C Dadswell cut his hand and was in contact with fluids therein. A steady officer, he did not panic but was glad to receive the ant-tetanus injection from Dr. Prentice, the police surgeon.

It transpired the young man in the casket had been killed in a road accident in Africa and had been a pal of mine from school when we walked home together most days. He was a cheerful happy soul but at least he'd come home.

Dr John Prentice was an old-fashioned Scottish bachelor general practitioner who had brought many of the town's babies into this life. A public spirited man he was closely involved with the St Johns Ambulance Brigade, sat on the bench of Magistrates and was very much involved as Police surgeon.

Before the advent of the breathalyser he attended every case where a suspect was thought to be driving under the influence of drink. The test by the doctor was a bit of a ritual. For instance the suspect had to walk down a white line marked on the floor, then to read a passage from the Christian Science Monitor, a free copy being delivered to the station for reasons unknown to the rank and file. Any paper would have done! Based on the tests by the doctor the driver was pronounced fit or unfit to drive.

One of these cases went to Quarter Sessions where the offender pleaded not guilty and Dr Prentice was called to the witness box and questioned by the accused's barrister who began as follows:-

"Dr Prentice I believed you are teetotal and have never been drunk in your life?"

"That's correct," said the doctor "

"Well," said the barrister, "Do you really think you are qualified to speak on drunkenness when you yourself have never been drunk?"

"Yes, your honour I do. I am also considered a leading authority on gynaecology and yet I've never had a baby!"

The barrister resumed his seat to the laughter of the entire court.

Chapter 9

Winter of 1962-3

Because there were no police houses available my wife and I had to find our own accommodation. Many of my fellow officers were in this position. We acquired a flat in Holy Trinity Vicarage, Lawkholme, in walking distance of the police station for which we were allowed £2 per week rent allowance. I suppose that helped the poor Vicar's stipend for wages were very low. A constable's pay was about £445 per year and to eke out most of our wives had jobs, mine working in Marks and Spencer's in Low Street.

I was a young boy during the 1947 winter and will never forget it. In fact I felt responsible for it. I loved snow and prayed for it. The trouble was it didn't know when to stop. The winter of 62-63 was similar. We had severe frosts and snow for weeks; the canal was frozen and the river in places; mountains of snow lay at the side of every road and animal foodstuffs were being air dropped by helicopters to livestock in the dales. The water was frozen and the only supply we had was from a tap deep in the church. Water bowsers were on the streets supplying the worst areas.

All the shifts were allowed back in the station every hour to get thawed out.

Whether it was the break-up of marriages or a legacy of the wars, there seemed to be many more vagrants and down-and-outs, some of these had served in the Boer War but mostly in the two World Wars. Throughout the fifties the British were involved in conflicts in Korea, the Middle East, Kenya, Malaya and Cyprus with young men from the town taking part in many of them as National Service conscripts for two years. Drugs had not yet entered the scene but alcohol was always available from the many public houses, clubs and off licences if you had the money. Finding former servicemen sleeping out in that winter was shameful but they were on the street and where else could they go but in the derelict houses all over the town?

One man had a different idea. He became like a Norwegian troll and lived under the bridge near the Fire Station down Coney Lane. He must have been as hard as nails and during the worst of that winter I feared I would find him dead yet he survived. He slept in cardboard boxes under a dry silted up arch of the ancient bridge. The centre arch spanned the river Worth which gave its name to the valley. It was not an ideal place and must have been running alive with rats at night.

When on the early shift I tried to patrol in that direction to check if he was still alive. Peering beneath the arch I could see he was not in his cardboard box then I spotted him. The river was deep frozen, covered in frost and snow and there he was standing on the thick ice. He's made a hole through it and was washing himself. Perhaps only in Russia in Tolstoy's 'War and Peace' would you have seen the likes of this. I asked him if he was alright and he nodded. It was rare for him to speak and clearly he had problems. If this had been Scotland and not Yorkshire the mere sleeping rough with nowhere to go meant he could be arrested.

When the thaw came and washed out his home he moved into an old house nearby. Still the recluse, he troubled no one until one night.

A young probationary constable was passing the old house. Hearing a noise he entered to be attacked by the troll who poked his fingers in the officer's eyes and ran away. Apart from the officer's night lamp there was little visibility and now he was temporarily blinded, needing help. A passer-by rang the station. The troll was arrested. The officer recovered.

The thaw caused other unexpected problems. Going off duty after the evening shift with two of my colleagues we made to cross the main road by the Hippodrome theatre. P.C. Harry Jeffrey, who I had shown round the beat for the first time after training school was from Cumberland and had worked in the steel works. The other chap was Eric Coates, a Geordie from the North East. Both had come south to 'better' themselves.

As we struggled through the deep slush we noticed an old lady across the road. She was very excited and shouting and waving to us, three Bobbies in full uniform.

"Take no notice of her, said Eric in his Geordie accent, "She's probably drunk."

The lady came across and pleaded with us to help her. It transpired she had a burst water pipe.

We trouped along with her to her house by the Drill Hall forgetting our wives would be wondering where we were. Harry's was with mine for company in the eerie vicarage.

The poor soul! The kitchen already had several inches of water on the floor and the pipe was pouring forth. Practical Harry soon stopped the leak and the three of us started clearing up with mops and buckets. Two hours later we set off for home again with the grateful thanks of the old lady warming our ears but we now had to convince our wives about the delay!

Next day I was on the carpet in front of Inspector Bolton Smith. A stolen car had been abandoned near to the Vicarage and according to him I had not seen it. Well, three police officers had walked passed it and failed to see it but I didn't tell him that, nor did I mention why we were too tired to notice after doing a good deed, worrying our wives and getting very late to bed.

"It won't happen again, Sir," I said, knowing full well that it likely would.

The thaw petered out and more heavy snowfalls occurred.

A report was received from the railway station that someone had stolen an electric trolley from the platform. This was very unusual. I accompanied Vic in the 999 response car but to no avail. Hardly had we returned to the police station when another report from the Gas Works said two men had just stolen a long wooden ladder. Again, this was odd but we set off again round the snow-covered streets. It was a regular blizzard now and the wind was causing drifting making driving hazardous. Fortunately there were few vehicles on the roads.

I had a hunch and asked Vic to drive along the longest street in town, Parkwood Street, which began near to the gas works. Unbelievably there it was, the trolley carrying the ladder. We pulled in, switched off the lights and waited. One man was guiding the trolley, the other steadying the ladder. They were totally engrossed in their task oblivious of our presence a bit like two of Scot's ill-fated arctic team with heads down against the icy wind and lashing snow-flakes.

As they came alongside Vic and I leapt out of the Westminster and both men ran for it. Vic grabbed one but mine ran up a steep street towards a wood which a wealthy Duke had once given the town. Weighed down with a heavy woollen greatcoat I was struggling and the man disappeared. All my family were hunters and I had been trained from early age to track my quarry. A rabbit or a hare was little different except rabbits, deer and hares had greater cunning and perhaps more intelligence than some human beings. Quietly following the man's fresh prints I tracked him into a small enclosed yard where he crouched by the wall of the coal-shed. I drew my staff just in case but he grinned saying it was a fair cop. Strangely enough in those days most criminals when caught came quietly. I knew why he grinned for I had caught these same two gambling in the street some weeks before but the charge was not accepted and I had to release them even though I knew the offence was valid. Now we had the pair of them on something more substantial.

It was agreed the trolley was technically a motor vehicle because it had an electric motor and they required a driving licence and insurance to take it on the road. Coupled with the offences of theft of the trolley and ladder it was an expensive outing when they appeared in court but at least we caught them before they commenced their burglary career with their mobile ladder for reaching up to windows!

Chapter 10

The finest building in town

The Mechanics Institute was without doubt the most majestic piece of architecture the poor old town of Keighley had. In a prominent position in the town centre it could be seen from north, south and west and many a bobby checked his watch by its large 'Big Ben' style clock. The building adjoined the Boys' Grammar School and the building itself was used for many civic functions including dances or more prestigious balls.

There was a dance on the fateful night and as I was working that beat Sergeant Haigh and I paid a routine visit to show the flag, as it were. The event was going nicely and there was a good atmosphere when suddenly from the bar end of the ballroom a group started singing. It was taken up by more and more. We grinned at one another for this had happened before. They were singing 'Old McDonald had a farm' but to their own words. Instead of McDonald they had substituted another 'Mac', a local policeman remembered with embarrassment by some senior police.

Within the County Forces it was very rare for an officer to go wrong despite the vastness of their area and the size of those county forces. The cities were much smaller and some had excellent reputations but not all. Of course it was a seven day wonder if a policeman broke the law, was arrested, brought before court and sent to jail but it happened in this rather unusual case.

Mac, as we shall call him was a former shepherd from Scotland coming south, like many others 'to better himself'. He was a likeable fellow and a good police officer. It seemed he had a future.

He kept a well-trained border collie which many of the local farmers wanted to buy. Sometimes he sold his dog to find it was waiting at home on his return.

Near his police house was a small field or paddock that no one appeared to be using until someone started to put sheep in it. Nothing was thought of this immediately but eventually it led to a police enquiry. Sheep were found ready for market in the police cellar when a search was ordered and the game was up for Mac who was charged with rustling or sheep stealing which once carried the death penalty. It was a big surprise for everyone and the police locally had to endure a lot of banter but all that passes with time. As we left that rowdy dance hall we did not realise it would be the last time we would set foot in there."

The next morning I was back on duty at six. I had to pass the Mechanics on the way to the police station. What a shame I thought as I saw all the fire engines, the smoke, the mass of hoses, some still being played on the ruined building whilst on the walls, the thick ice formed as the water touched the stone. It was a sad but spectacular sight and it led to the demise of the best building in town. Was it arson or a dropped light, as the fire brigade call it? Who knows! A rubbishy edifice was built to replace it, symptomatic of the shoddy times we were entering with ever falling standards in civic pride.

"At least our former enemies in Germany were able to rebuild whole towns bombed by the allies at the allies' expense," commented several old soldiers from the Duke of Wellington's regiment, "Did we really win the war?"

Thinking of rogue police officers brings to mind an incident that occurred at the start of the Second World War when a detective sergeant became aware of corruption involving senior officers concerning food which was rationed and in short supply. He kept a dossier on the suspects and was just about to blow the whistle on them when they got wind of his plans and arranged for him to get his call-up papers. He in turn was tipped off by a colleague. Wasting no time he took his file and went to Westgate station in Wakefield, taking a train to London. He went straight to the Home Office and presented his file.

This matter resulted in the resignation of several very senior officers but because of the likely damage to morale in wartime no other action was taken. I gather the detective sergeant was not promoted further. Some thought him a brave man to expose this. Certainly it was patriotic in the wartime conditions where the bulk of the population were living on very meagre rations but it carried great personal risks as every whistle blower knows.

In Victoria Park museum in addition to the mummy there was always on display a set of Irish bagpipes, believed 'Coin' make, the bag covered in a Campbell tartan which was not unusual for there were many Campbells in Ireland. As a piper they fascinated me from an early age. When Cliff Castle was set up they were moved into a glass display cabinet up there, available for viewing by everyone. On Burns Night the museum was broken into and the pipes were the only item stolen. This cast suspicion on someone wanting to use them for copying for they were an ancient set and there was a revival in Irish bagpipes at that time and one or two people were making them locally. However, despite enquiries the pipes were never recovered. To steal anything from a museum set up to educate the public is a rotten thing to do but no one escapes the consequences of their actions. The pity is they don't see that before they commit the crime!

A gang of burglars operating from a house in Worth Village near the hollow were causing havoc to shops, clubs and other business premises. P.C. Geoff Turton the Parkwood man, Les Allinson, the Riddlesden man, Lance Turner from CID and myself from the town had been detailed to catch them and bring an end to the pillaging.

We knew who the gang were and where they lived. They had a van and we knew about that so we watched and waited for them to set off. The idea was for me to travel with PC Allinson in his 'Baby Austin'. Now Les was a big, burly ex-military policeman and he took up a lot of room so when the van took off there was a slight delay in our departure and we lost sight of them.

We then re-joined our colleagues at the thieves den and the four of us concealed ourselves and waited. It was so much like a military exercise trying to catch terrorists which we were all experienced in.

The van arrived back very late, pulling up at the door of the back-to-back house, then we swooped giving none of them time to realise what was happening. Each man was banged up against the wall with legs apart and handcuffed behind his back, searched then taken to the van. It was full of thousands of cigarettes, alcohol, stand pies, boxes of blue ribbon biscuits and hams, sides of beef, chickens, turkeys, a proverbial Aladdin's cave.

The four men were crammed in with their loot for we had no other transport and no radios in those days. PC Turton would drive the van with P.C. Turner and Les would drive his own car with me as passenger behind the van. Suddenly the van door flew open and out jumped the ringleader who's slipped his cuffs. He ran to his house door banging as hard as he could with his fist. There appeared his lady, a real harridan who immediately began screaming at us with language which would have made the cat blush. We replaced her husband back in the van and went on our way.

When safely locked in the cells I was given the job of listing all the stolen property and finding its value for the charges, no mean task! Seeing the hams and stand pies laid out on the table reminded me of a true story from 1914 when news of the First World War came to Keighley and anti-German sentiment was ignited among some of the townsfolk. Hoffman's Pork butchers in Church Green had been long established and accepted in the town until the war when the shop was sacked by the mob and all the foodstuffs stolen including hams and stand pies. Of course this was long before my time but one day whilst walking up Hospital Road, Riddlesden, I was shown by a local man, himself a boy at the time, where the stand pies and hams etc. had been hidden!

The Mechanics Institute, Keighley. Photograph by Mr Hargreaves, courtesy of Keighley News

Chapter 11

Isn't It Quiet!

Very little money had ever been spent on the town police station. In its day it had been the rather grand residence of the local Chief Superintendent but gradually it was taken over to accommodate the various departments of uniform, CID and the small police women's branch. The mess room where we had our tea and sandwiches was a sort of afterthought. It comprised a gas oven, sink, long table bearing a 999 phone and dining chairs that had seen better days.

This particular night our shift was having its supper break in the early hours. Sandy, covering an outside beat had cycled in to collect his correspondence and a catch-up. A card game was in progress. Someone said "Isn't it quiet!" a number of voices said, "Don't ever say that!" The young officer coloured up at the reaction, picking up a magazine. Within less than a minute the 999 telephone on the table rang its demanding notes.

"Go on, pick the bloody thing up," said Vic impatient at his game being disturbed.

The latest recruit picked up the receiver. "A woman's been shot through the eye. She's at the phone box by the Volunteers," he said in one breath.

The room erupted as one with men grabbing their helmets, fastening their tunics and running for the door. Sandy's bike came useful that night with him riding it and Sergeant Harry Spedding sitting behind, legs out to left and right, his cape billowing behind like Batman. MacMillan and I ran all the way and were the first to arrive at Lawkholme Lane followed by the sergeant still on the bike. The poor woman had indeed been shot in the eye and was still bleeding. She told us her husband was armed and out. We took that to mean on the loose with a pistol.

The Austin Westminster at last arrived after its usual playing up session and with the sergeant, Vic, McMillan and I we sped to the scene of the shooting. McMillan, a tough Lowland Scot recently released from the military went forward to the house, each of us with our staffs drawn. There was a small yard at the back door and the gate was open. We listened and could hear deep breathing. Mac cautiously approached the door which was slightly ajar. Very slowly he pushed it wide enough to see inside. I joined him. A man lay on the carpet with a serious gun-shot wound to the head and a .22 pistol by his side but despite the dreadful injury he was still alive. Vic radioed from the car for another ambulance. There was nothing else we could do but wait. This was a crime scene, certainly attempted murder.

The man was taken to hospital with an officer to sit by his bedside in case he recovered and made a dying declaration but he passed away in the night.

He had been a member of a shooting club which required a simple firearms certificate costing a few shillings. A family dispute had led to tragedy once the gun came into play. Had the gun not been there it is likely matters would have been settled without harm.

It took Dunblane and Hungerford to bring about draconian measures in the control of hand guns yet the criminal fraternity still have them and use them. We've travelled a long way since Craig and Bentley where a gun was used and a man was hanged and the death penalty abolished. Never have we had so many lawyers prosecuting, defending, sitting in judgement yet we seem to have forgotten the law should be an awesome thing, there to keep everyone on the straight and narrow with dire consequences for those who transgress. There are no dire consequences and today a court sentencing a man to prison risks turning him into a monster just for having been there. There are better ways of reducing crime but would any government dare to implement it. It is almost as though they have a vested interest in preserving the status quo – I wonder why?

To investigate and detect crime one needs dedicated officers. Much of today's crime committed against ordinary people is not investigated. Give them an inch they'll take a yard, the saying goes but if someone takes the law into their own hand in defending their property the law will squash them flat. The scales are the symbol of Justice; have they not been tilted a little too heavily in one direction?

Sergeant Harry Spedding was the youngest of our sergeants and well liked for his fairness, intelligence, and sense of humour. He quickly rose to Chief Inspector then died suddenly, a great loss, for the police service needed his likes. Whilst in charge of our shift he persuaded me to be the Divisional Correspondent for the White Rose, the force journal. Brian Midgley was the editor but when he went to university my friend Barry Shaw became editor and I became assistant editor. This meant trips to headquarters for various meetings and an opportunity to mix with senior officers on equal terms, always of course with deference due!

On my last meeting with Harry he told me of a trip to the Strid with his family and how they posed for a remote photograph from the camera on a tripod. As they waited and watched the tripod slowly tilted over and fell into the Strid, camera and all.

Harry also encouraged me to study for the law examinations and so I began to take studying seriously.

P.C Shaw and I became good friends and I taught him to shoot and having a number of children he was able to take plenty of rabbits and other game home for Rosie to cook for police pay was still not great.

Barry wrote several books for writing was his real interest. He also did book reviews and built up a fine library giving me one or two I had an interest in such as T.E Lawrence's 'Seven Pillars of Wisdom' covering areas of the Levant where my father served in WW2.

When visiting his home near Tadcaster I noticed a vase full of peacock feathers and asked where they came from. He was not forthcoming but said he'd tell me one day. I kept him to his word and he eventually told me the tale of him shooting pigeons at dusk on an estate where he had shooting rights. Whilst standing beneath a large Oak tree the biggest pheasant he had ever seen flew out from above him and he instinctively shot it. It fell on the drive to the castle and his dog ran immediately to pick it up but refused and danced round the dead bird barking its head off as if a calamity had occurred, which it had!

On reaching home he persuaded Rosie that it was not a peacock as she said, but some sort of pheasant. He even produced all the British Bird books to prove his case but in the end she convinced him of his dreadful deed. The bird was in his boot for a week before it was returned to its home and the fox got the blame. The feathers, however, were admired for many a year!

Barry suffered a stroke at 40 and died. He was another irreplaceable officer but at least he got the Force Newspaper off the ground during his editorship.

Being a countryman it soon became accepted that I would deal with birds, animals and reptiles. Keighley is not renowned for its reptiles but a call from up Devonshire Street had Vic send me thence to deal with a snake a boy had found. Now in the highlands working with ponies we killed adders on sight for biting the ponies' feet and I had done the same out riding on Luneburg Heath in Germany but this snake had me puzzled. It was quite large, had a nice pattern down its length and although it didn't seem poisonous, I wasn't sure. I persuaded the boy to escort me to the station carrying his find.

The only receptacle I could find to place it in was a waste-paper basket and on this I placed a heavy law book (Stones Justices' Manual) to secure it. The young lad departed and I was wishing he'd never found it. It was my intention to release it up by the tarn where it might have a chance of finding a mate. Unfortunately, when I returned to the parade room the book had been removed and the snake had gone. There was uproar but in spite of a diligent search it was never found. Whether it got under the floorboards and like a toad lived on whatever insects it could find I'll never know but the incident was soon forgotten, but could it still be resident there?

The firm of Dean Smith and Grace on Parkwood Street was hardly the place to find a mink yet one of their employees, Albert Smith, of Peck wood caught one with his bare hands in the work shop and brought it in a box to the police station. Mink are renowned for being vicious and this was showing those characteristics as it was left with me deciding what to do with it. The mink farms were not interested for fear of having claims against them from poultry breeders and so the unfortunate wee creature went back to the finder who was used to handling ferrets and he despatched it humanely holding it behind the neck with his bare hand, something I would not have done!

Chapter 12

POSB

Post Office Savings Bank Books were a common method of saving but they had their flaws and were vulnerable to thieves. I knew this from experience when a pal had his stolen from his locker when we were stationed in Dover. However, a pattern emerged when the thief started withdrawing money at sub-post offices in London and the suspect became apparent for he lived in that area; others who had access to our barrack room lived in the north. We knew it would not be easy to catch him without someone going to London at the weekends and because of our other duties we couldn't do that.

Just before lights out after the pipes had finished playing we dragged him from his bed and took him to the shower-room. It was quickly made clear why he was there and he was given the opportunity to confess as the level of water in the cold bath increased. He did confess, the book was returned and he agreed to repay the money out of his army pay. The gypsy's warning has its uses, sometimes even in Civvies Street but it must be used sparingly for not all do-gooders approve! A case of does the end justify the means. I am afraid sometimes it does. In all disciplined organisations mutual respect is essential just as it was in school where the big swishy cane hung like the sword of Damocles.

A Polish man came to report an almost identical case of his Post Office Savings Book being stolen from his home along by the Catholic Church. I accompanied him to his neat terraced house, noticing the crucifix on the wall and photographs of him in uniform. I asked him about his homeland and the tears came to his eyes. I promised him I would get his life savings back and went to see Charlie, the desk sergeant.

When the Nazis invaded Poland Britain declared war on Germany. The Poles fought hard for their homeland charging modern tanks with cavalry armed with lances and sabres. Those that escaped to Britain fought with the Royal Air Force during the battle of Britain helping to prevent invasion; others fought at Casino and with the Airborne at Arnhem. We had respect for those people.

Sergeant Charlie Robinson had lost his hand on the Normandy beaches and there were times one could see it still gave him pain yet he was brilliant at running the office and could hold two telephones at once, one in his good hand the other squeezed up near his ear with his shoulder. He could be taciturn and when I asked if I could go on plain-clothes duty for three days to try to recover the Pole's money I was amazed when he agreed. He looked at me with his steely grey eyes and I knew he didn't think I would succeed.

Visiting all the sub-post offices I found the one where the withdrawals were being made and the approximate times. There began a waiting game which paid off on my third day. Marching the culprit through the town to the police station was very satisfying but more so when I wheeled him through Charlie's office to be charged. I think that was when Charlie's attitude towards me changed for he started to entrust me with some risky ventures escorting prisoners.

We were always short of men for the shifts due to courses, sickness or court appearances. He didn't have an easy job but he was clever at manipulating numbers. We all had the greatest respect for him and his war service and went out of our way not to annoy him.

"I want you to get into plain clothes and go to Birmingham to collect a prisoner," he announced one morning. He gave no information as to who the prisoner was or for what he was wanted on warrant for. The journey was uneventful and I arrived in New Street station at lunch time. It was a short walk to the police station where I signed for the prisoner.

"Is there another officer with you?" asked the custody officer.

"No," I said, "Just me."

The custody officer cleared his throat and said, "Well, you'd better take a look at him," leading me to the cells. Before going in he whispered, "He is a freedom fighter from Hungary so be careful he's a big chap."

He seemed twice my height, spoke broken English and couldn't understand what all the fuss was about."

I handcuffed him to my left wrist and draped my raincoat over it. The City police had driven us to the station and now we sat in the compartment, my charge up against the window.

The Hungarian rising began in 1956 when Britain took in thousands of refugees fleeing from the Russians. I told him that year I had occupied a barracks in Dover in which the refugees had stayed before my battalion moved in on return from Cyprus. I commented that I knew the Magyars were brave fighters similar to the highlanders. He became quite animated and kept the conversation going until Leeds. It transpired he had been in the very same barracks we had but I didn't say anything about the mess we had to clear up.

Back at my own station I placed the prisoner in the cell, got him a meal and went to see Charlie. He seemed surprised to see me back so quickly. Like the Birmingham police he knew I was taking a risk escorting a prisoner alone for normally two officers were used. He must have thought I could be trusted not to allow him to escape but you never knew for certain with Charlie.

"Did you know he was a Hungarian freedom fighter, Sergeant?" I asked.

"No," he replied, "And he didn't know he was cuffed to a Gordon Highlander but you got him here."

"Out of curiosity, what is his offence?" I asked.

"Failing to pay £2 for a parking ticket," said the Sergeant, hurrying out of my presence.

It was true; the absurdity of it; the expense of the time and the rail journey. British Justice could be just a little silly at times. I would have paid £2 not to have gone but even this was part of the training!

Some days one could patrol the beat for the whole tour without being disturbed by lawless behaviour. Such days were rare but not wasted bringing opportunities to talk to tradesman, shopkeepers and passers-by. Much was learned from these people for the town was generally pro-police. There was also time to notice things like the trout in the North Beck below Oakworth Road and the mature almond nut tree nearby. That tree had masses of pink blossoms in the spring and pollinated by the bees produced lots of excellent almond nuts in the autumn, a treat during night patrols. Alas the tree was cut down by the Council. I don't suppose they even knew what it was.

One morning, outside Willis Walker's I noticed a willow warbler lying apparently dead against the shop wall. It was a cold April morning and I knew the bird had just arrived back from Africa so on the chance it was still alive I cupped it in my warm hands. Sure enough it was alive and after an hour in the warmth of the police station I took it to Devonshire Park and released it. Any bird that travels from Africa to Keighley deserves to live!

My uncle, John Holt, served in the North African campaign at Tobruk during the war and now worked for Timothy Taylor at the Ingrow brewery. He said this of his German captors: "I was very ill and not expected to live and if it hadn't been for an ordinary German soldier carrying me for medical attention and keeping me fed I would have died. Also, when we got to the camp in Germany an old lady came each morning and pushed a basket of bread under the wire, so don't think they were all bad."

Johnny's Grandfather John Holt, master mason and monumental sculpture who after moving from Holt in Norfolk to Skipton settled in Keighley and is credited with building the gates to Cliff Castle and working on the stonework in the construction of Ponden reservoir. He carried out intricate stonework on churches and cathedrals up and down the country, travelling with two cases, one containing his tools, the other a large fruit cake to sustain him.

Johnny's uncle Zac was killed in the South African war and another Uncle Charlie was wounded. Johnny's father also served there in the Mounted Infantry. Zac's name is in the Parish Church, another refuge for a weary night duty constable for in those days the doors were always open, as churches should be!

Other members of the Holt family were founder members of the Independent Labour Party in the town swayed by speeches by Kier Hardy, Jimmy Maxton and Phillip Snowden, all desperate to see living conditions improve.

Another John Holt, my grandfather's brother, immigrated to New Zealand from Morton in 1906, taking his wife, children and mistress. He travelled with another radical who was later knighted by the Queen. He wrote to his sister working in a Keighley mill and said,

"For God's sake, get out of that town!" Emma went to America and thrived.

He lived in Christchurch until nearly a hundred and the radical knight read the eulogy at his funeral. John, of Keighley stock is remembered by some for riding a horse up the steps of the government building in Christchurch on some legitimate protest. They don't make them in Keighley like that anymore!

Another good friend I made at Keighley was Bob Walbank of Oakworth Road. Bob was an engineer at Stells' Tube Mill up Fell Lane. He knew my family had connections with the Royal Scots and introduced me to his father a Royal Scot during WW1 who also was captured by the Germans in France. After interrogation he was given sandwiches and put on a train for Germany with a number of other prisoners of war but then separated and sent unescorted on another train up into North Germany where he was met by a farmer with a horse and cart and a shot gun. They drove for a great distance arriving eventually at the farm where the farmer placed the gun back on the wall saying, "There will be no more need of that. Now this is your home until it's over."

His capture by the Germans likely saved his life without which his son Bob and his children we would never have known and that strong Yorkshire line would have died out!

Bob and his brother Jack both served during WW2 and Jack was involved in heavy fighting a Caen in Normandy but survived the war. His son Geoff unearthed the largest haul of Celtic gold coins near Silsden. Excellent copies are on display in Cliffe Castle, the originals are in the British Museum.

Chapter 13

Who Dares Wins

A young cadet by the name of Terry Slocombe was posted to the Division and on his first day as a probationary constable he was put with me to learn the beat. He'd spent some time in the office where Desk Charlie had given him the run around. If the sergeant apparently thought little of us this pale-faced immature teenage ex-cadet received little encouragement. How wrong could Charlie have been?

A little while after that this young man was up on the hills on the outskirts of the town with his girlfriend when he saw a suspicious van with a gang of equally suspicious ruffians. He saw they were trying to open a safe. Sending his girlfriend to get police help he watched from a distance as the light was fading. Concerned that reinforcements might be too late, bearing in mind he was in civilian clothes, he crept close to them as they struggled with the safe then ran at them shouting, "I am a police officer, you are all under arrest. The whole group surrendered to him as the police cars arrived.

This incident was the start of an outstanding career. This young man had shown great courage. He had not been in the SAS but he had been a first class Scout and clearly there was something special about him for he went on to be awarded the British Empire Medal for disarming a gunman then the Queen's Gallantry Medal for saving lives at the Bradford Fire and finished up a Divisional Commander still raising money for the Scout Movement. Charlie would have been very proud of him!

Two former London ladies who helped to keep the show on the road as telephone receptionists at the police station were Nora Peggs and Paddy. The Peggs family had arrived at the Murder House in Riddlesden during the war after enemy action in Croydon, Mr Peggs working at the NSF factory in Ingrow. They never quite lost that cockney accent but their sons Gordon and Geoff soon became Yorkshire men and were proud of it.

One Riddlesden chum, when he became a teenager, led the police a dance and is the only person I know of in Keighley who was arrested for going about with his face blackened or disguised with intent to commit an offence under the Vagrancy Act, 1824, an Act brought in to control wounded soldiers back from the Napoleonic wars who were roaming the land destitute and starving, complete with campaign medals awarded by Wellington. I gather some of them thought more of Napoleon than their own Commander!

A relative of mine Sammy Unwin, who had served in the Great War, regularly preached Socialism in the town hall square and regularly was locked up for his audacity and dedication to his beliefs. Other relatives would bail him out but from what he had seen in the war and the events in Russia, he knew things had to improve for the masses. He spoke a lot of sense and is still remembered as a brilliant orator by those who knew him.

One night I was called to St. Ann's Church opposite the Picture House cinema where the resident priest had caught a youth stealing from the offertory box in the church. The priest was a fine strapping Irishman with more than a modicum of common-sense for he had done something I was forbidden to do and I am sure the young man would remember it the rest of his days and hopefully he would not steal again. Sufficient to say Justice was done!

Whilst in the church I asked to look at the memorial stone for the Great War where one of my Uncles Hugh Cobrey, The Kings Own Scottish Borderers was killed in 1917 in his twenties. He was born of Scotto-Irish parents in Keighley off West Lane. His brother was wounded the same day in the local Duke of Wellingtons Regiment in which a further brother John served.

St. Mary's Anglican Church in Dalton Lane was a beautiful building of intricately carved stone. Had it survived the massacre of Keighley's churches it would be a listed building today and no doubt put to good use. Many of my family were married there and it happened to be where I was christened. My friend, Albert Smith climbed the Dalton Mill chimney unaided just to look at a kestrel's nest near the church.

During the big depression of the 30s Albert had been out at night long-netting rabbits and returning to his home at Parkwood via the snicket alongside St. Mary's he was challenged by the Parkwood Bobbie who had been waiting to catch him.

Albert told the constable he had caught the rabbits on Alderman Tack's land at Riddlesden. The officer gave him until noon that day to produce written consent from the Alderman.

Alderman Tack was sympathetic to Albert's story knowing of the massive unemployment in the town and how the rabbits would go to help feed the poor so he gave written consent. The constable was very surprised at the turn of events for he really thought he had caught Albert for poaching. During the war Albert served in the Merchant Navy and was extremely brave in saving another sailor's life thanks to his climbing skills practised on the Dalton Mill chimney.

A contingent of strong men from Keighley police station were required to go to Saddleworth Moor off the M62 to search for the bodies of missing children buried there by the infamous duo Brady and Hindley. The officers were digging in wet peat over a vast area with few clues to go on and it was hard physical work. They returned filthy and exhausted yet were ready for the resumption of the task the next day. Some of those children were never found despite a long drawn-out search. This murder enquiry was perhaps the worst of any we had heard of at that time and started to make some of us rethink on our attitude towards the death penalty so recently abolished!

A young boy was murdered as he was fishing on the Leeds and Liverpool canal at Bingley. The man was eventually captured at Matlock in Derbyshire. After completing his prison sentence he was released and killed a girl.

The commandments tell us: 'Thou shalt not kill' which puts the so called Christian State in a dilemma since hanging was abolished and the ultimate deterrent was removed from the Statute Book yet human beings continue to kill one another at an accelerated pace or at least it seems so. The so called 'do gooders' won't hear of a return to the death penalty nor to any other means of painless execution. Rather they would see such violent offenders incarcerated for the rest of their days at continued risk and astronomic cost to the law-abiding people when such cost could be put to better use.

The purpose of law is mainly to deter not punish. Today's punishment does not deter the really bad but makes them more cunning and difficult to bring to justice.

When dealing with dangerous animals we do not hesitate in putting them down humanely then the threat is gone. A more enlightened society would have found a satisfactory solution to the problem by now. Only in a war situation are young men encouraged to take the life of the opposing side by any means even though they have no personal grudge against them yet some of the most abhorrent criminals in history are kept incarcerated at huge expense and risk of escape to offend again.

Always there are those who say "What if we execute the wrong person?" Surely if a humane death penalty works and saves many lives, the odd mistake can be considered unfortunate but for the common good!

At a remote railway station called Oxenhome, in what was Cumberland; two police officers were shot dead in the 60s. Superintendent Mogg in charge of an adjoining Division of the West Riding sent armed reinforcements and attended the scene himself. There occurred something that is very rare in law-enforcement circles when a Hue and Cry, a mediaeval gathering of police and local men, all armed, began a huge sweep of the countryside. In the course of the search the offender was shot.

It seems there is little hope of the death penalty being introduced and so we will continue having accelerating homicide rates until all police officers carry firearms as part of the routine just to protect themselves and the public will have to grin and bear it unless all the law-abiding ones apply for firearm certificates as well. Now there's a thought! America here we come!

Chapter 14

Rape and Quarter Sessions

'These allegations are easy to make, hard to prove but still harder to disprove'. These are the words of the Lord Chief Justice and they are equally true today concerning the offence of rape.

Sergeant Tom Haigh came looking for me in the mess room. " We've just had a rape reported and there are no CID men available. Would you deal with it?"

"Of course," I answered.

"That's settled then and you already know the suspect because you've arrested him before for dishonesty!"

The offence had been committed against a 12 year old girl and reported by her mother. My first task was to arrange for the victim to be examined by a doctor then to have her statement taken by a Woman Police Officer. Whilst this was going on the sergeant and I visited the scene. I found an open penknife on the floor of the bedroom where the offence allegedly occurred and collected a ten shilling note from the mother. This had been given to the girl immediately after the offence by the suspect. We then went in search of the offender.

Finding him at his home, I cautioned him, told him the nature of the offence and that I was arresting him.

At the police station he was placed in a bare room, stood on a sheet and ordered to strip. Each garment was placed in a bag for forensic examination. Vic stood guard by the door watching the procedure and making sure I missed nothing this being the first serious sex offence I had dealt with.

At length the pathetic figure stood naked, his hands shielding his front, embarrassed, uncomfortable and shaking. I handed him a white suit to put on. It was at that moment Vic decided to speak. Until then had said not a word.

"Did you enjoy it then?" he asked inappropriately. The prisoner looked at Vic not knowing what to say then a sly smile seemed to gather about his mouth.

"You bastard," said Vic forcefully, as he turned and left the room. If the man wasn't shaking before he was now.

The committal in the Magistrates Court ran smoothly, Superintendent Verity presenting the case which would be heard at the next Quarter Sessions at Wakefield. The accused was remanded in custody.

It was always a fine sunny day when I had to attend court and it seemed such a waste when I could be out in the fresh air. I knew I would come away with a headache for I always did. Perhaps it was the atmosphere or the electric lights or more likely the angry words between cross-examining lawyers and the accused or sometimes the Bench. Maybe it was the sight of the offenders, some obviously ill, poor, down at heel, without hope and the other kind, confident, well dressed, cocky, loud, sure they could wheedle their way out of yet another appearance for dishonestly taking advantage of their fellow-men.

Wakefield was quite a smart clean city; the centre for the West Riding. A fine war memorial stood at the gates to Police Headquarters commemorating those officers who had paid the ultimate sacrifice in the wars.

On entering the Quarter Sessions I was introduced to the barrister presenting the case and put at ease. It was to be a guilty plea but I was questioned in the witness box by the barristers and the Judge. The accused stood forlorn in the dock. Perhaps he was still thinking of what Vic had called him.

"This is the worst case of this kind that has ever come before me," said the Judge "You will go to prison for eighteen months, I wish it were longer."

The charge had been reduced from Rape to one of sexual intercourse with a girl under thirteen. The lawyers had thought the charge of rape could not be proved. I think the Judge thought otherwise. No matter it was over and I had to get back to my station.

The defending solicitor Mr Scott was known to me and kindly agreed to run me back in his fine sports car which spared me the otherwise uncomfortable journey of changing busses or trains. It was a kindly gesture. We did not discuss the case.

On another occasion a teenage girl reported she had been raped at a certain youth club by two boys her own age. After being interviewed she acknowledged she had exaggerated; that the boys had merely touched her. When the boys were interviewed by me and a detective sergeant they claimed she had flirted with them and encouraged them to chase her.

They confessed to having touched her with her approval. In law, under a certain age, approval could not be given and this was always a tricky one with sexually aware teenagers. The boys were quite open and honest about what had taken place and made aware of how easily they could have had a conviction for indecent assault but otherwise, no further action was taken.

Half the teenage population would end up being charged and that would not be right. Within a couple of years some girl would delight at 'being touched' by either of them. At least they didn't get a black mark for life which could have spoiled things for them seriously. The girl too was reprimanded for her false claims!

Chapter 15

The Seaforth Highlander

Just before Christmas I dealt with a theft from a boarding house up near the hospital. A Scotsman who had been staying there was suspected of taking some £60 pounds. It was believed he had returned to Scotland where his wife and children were living and his details were transmitted to the Scottish Police.

Charlie the sergeant beckoned me into his office.

"Glasgow police have arrested your thief and I want you to go and fetch him back for appearance in court in the morning."

There was no argument whatever my own arrangements with my wife might have been. I got my travel warrant, put on a civvy raincoat and went to catch my train.

"We'll let your wife know," were the sergeant's last words.

When I arrived at the police station in Glasgow and identified myself. Two huge burley Jocks looked at me and said, "You're not by yourself, are you?"

I informed them I was. Clearly they were not used to this West Riding austerity.

"Well, you'd better cuff him and watch him like a hawk for he was a Seaforth Highlander."

"Aye," I replied, "Well tell him it's a Gordon Highlander who's come to take him."

The Glasgow police were very courteous and ran me across to Buchanan Street Station to meet one of my army pals from the West Highlands. I had been his best man. The reunion was brief but it made the trip North more worthwhile.

I handcuffed the prisoner and was about to get into the police car when a sergeant from the property department said, "You'll want the evidence!"

He handed me a large cardboard box containing a doll and an even larger Teddy bear.

"He's spent all the money on presents for his kids for Christmas. He's out of work and went down to England to try and get a job. The poor beggar's desperate."

They dropped the pair of us at the railway station. I covered his wrists with the boxed doll and carried the huge Teddy bear under my arm, holding on to him with my other. Once aboard I put him near the window and warned him about escaping for the temptation must have been great to get back to his family.

"Now understand this Caber Feidh," (His regimental motto). I said, "If you try anything I will be obliged to take severe action and you ken what that will be." He nodded.

I really felt sorry for this highlander who had fallen on bad times. I knew the Seaforth's well; they were a good regiment and any one of us might have been in his situation. Actually, we got on famously, were able to speak a little in the Gaelic and of course in this small world he knew people I knew in the piping fraternity.

At Dumfries the lights on the train failed and we were plunged into darkness. The prisoner assured me he would not misbehave. We travelled all the way to Carlisle in pitch darkness and had to disembark until the lights were restored. I put my raincoat over his hand to hide the cuffs, piled him up with the Teddy bear and carried the doll myself whilst holding his arm. Despite being shackled it would have been so easy to make a run for it but the fight had gone out of him and that was sad to see in one who had served the Crown propping up the fading Empire and endured so much for the Common Good.

We had tea and cakes in the restaurant until the train was ready then resumed our journey without incident.

It was in the early hours of the morning that we arrived back at the station. An officer told me my wife had been up looking for me when I was missing for so long. Charlie had forgotten to tell her I was on escort. Well, he was a very busy man. I prepared the file for court at 10 am and snatched a few hours' sleep.

The court took heed about what I said. They too had some sympathy and being his first offence allowed him to keep the presents for his children but he had to return the money at so much a week. Now the poor chap had to repeat his journey to Glasgow and he had not a bawbee but being so near Christmas there was still some goodwill in the poor old town and the Guardian Angel of the Seaforth Highlanders was watching over him. We parted on good terms and I wished him well. I hope he was never so impoverished again.

At Haworth lived an interesting constable who was half Scottish, very public spirited and very agreeable company. He also was a good musician and knew his Robert Burns poetry. However, a bit like Michael Crawford in 'Some mothers do have 'em' he sometimes landed in situations!

Whilst patrolling the outlying districts of the Division in the 999 car somewhere between the hours of four and five a.m. the car collided with a wall. This is a very dangerous time for such officers who by then are getting very sleepy.

When such an incident occurred it was nearly always the same 'black and white collie dog' that ran across the road causing the driver to swerve. In this officer's case it was claimed to be 'a low flying duck'!

Superintendent Mogg was heard to ask "Wasn't the dog good enough?"

Chapter 16

Duncan

Duncan was a good friend, a first class police officer and a family man. He came from the border country where he had worked on a large farm as a shepherd. Trusty and reliable he had a little of Robert Burns about him. His wife was a gem from the same area; a very intelligent and athletic lady. It was not long before Duncan was off my shift and put in charge of a desirable outside beat.

Outside beats were the same as anywhere else except the resident officer generally had to deal with everything that occurred from criminal offences, deaths, found dogs, domestic disputes and road accidents. Sandy was good at his job and much respected.

It was domestic dispute that led to his downfall, something that could happen to anyone for they were common enough. Usually when the bobby attended, often at the instigation of the wife, the couple would mysteriously join forces venting their spleen against the officer. Couples can be very strange when confronted by authority.

In this case the marriage was clearly over and Duncan called at the house from time to time to see her ex was not troubling her. The inevitable happened and they became fond of one another.

Word reached CID that a contract had been put out to deal with Duncan and he was recalled to work in the office for his own safety. He felt humiliated and angry but the Chief would not take the risk of allowing him to work his normal shifts so he resigned and disappeared from the scene eventually marrying the lady.

This was a loss to the Police Force and to the friends he left. No one knew where he was then we learned that he'd passed away.

It is not just constables this can happen to. Senior officers comforting police widows can sometimes become involved; risks that go with the job, I suppose! The test, when this happens is surely to put both families first and try not to hurt anyone, something easier said than done but many have the strength to do it.

Another Jock who landed on the carpet was on plain-clothes duty in South Yorkshire when he was bitten three times by dogs in one week. This man was from the industrial belt of Scotland and had served in the Korean War in the

Black Watch, the Royal Highland Regiment. He was a tough guy but with a heart of gold. It was a hard war in a hostile environment and the winters were harsh. Many British lives were lost and one of Jock's pals was killed alongside him during a mortar attack by the enemy. You could not have a better man beside you in a rough house. This is the story of how he became a beat bobby on a very rough housing estate on the outskirts of town known as 'Devil's Island'.

Jock was on plain-clothes duty and bitten three times by dogs in a week. He was incensed more with the dog owners than their savage pets.

"Oh officer, he's never done that before, can I wipe the blood off your leg."

Jock was so fed up with this business that he swore the next dog to bite him he would split its skull and he did, right in front of the owner. You can imagine the fuss but at least it wasn't the irresponsible owner's skull he'd cracked.

It is agreed that anyone else would have got the sack but not Jock. He was too useful and to Devil's Island he was sent where he made a big impression on the inhabitants and restored law and order and although he was still bitten by dogs going about his duty he never killed another. As he would say it wasn't the dog's fault.

Jock was hot-blooded and when called before the Inspector for some minor misdemeanour, the Inspector unwisely overstepped the mark when upbraiding him. Jock simmered, his military discipline holding firm but the Inspector added even greater insult so the worthy constable smacked him and knocked him to the ground. There were no witnesses but Jock was posted to a beat which, compared with Bracken Bank was just pure heaven!

It was there he was as useful as ever maintaining order and saving life.

Chapter 17

The Charnel House

It was the duty of the police to accept and deal with found dogs. These were removed to kennels on the outskirts of town and kept for ten days. If they hadn't been claimed within that time the police took them to the RSPCA to be 'put down'! There were a lot of dogs in the town, frequently a nuisance, especially when they roamed in packs for the wolf is in all canine breeds and some farmers shot them on sight if they even looked at a sheep. Many were undernourished and diseased with mange and distemper from neglect.

No officer liked to take dogs to be destroyed but everyone had to take their turn. It was not a pleasant task. The small branch of the RSPCA was in a terraced cottage in Starkey Street. It was run by Hilda Stell a little old lady who was stronger than she looked both in constitution and physically.

There were seven dogs for execution this day and she made me aware of how the system worked. Each dog was taken one at a time into the building. Some of the lads called it the Charnel House, for such it was. Hilda fitted an electrode to each ear and pressed a switch. There was the smell of singing hair and the dog dropped to the floor, quite dead, still twitching from the nerves like the many wild creatures I had killed. Some of the dogs were large and she needed a hand dragging them into the yard outside to await the glue van's regular collection. It was sickening really for some dogs would have been some child's pet and they were all so trusting throughout the procedure.

I confess it occurred to me that this form of execution was so very simple compared with hanging which was still in vogue but not as quick then my thoughts went back to my visit to the Military hospital at Belsen and the concentration camp nearby with the mass graves, remembering the films our officers showed us who were some of the first to enter that Charnel House!

Some 'found' dogs brought to the police station by well-meaning 'do gooders' were never lost at all and when put on a lead by a constable would, with a wag of the tail, cheerfully lead him home, sometimes a short distance away! We hated seeing good dogs put down but this was the system and no wonder it was kept quiet!

I am sure Miss Stell did not like this aspect of her work but it was part of her duty as it was ours and we didn't like it either. She spent her life caring for and healing animals and birds and provided valuable service to the town. I remember her being instrumental in tightening up the rules on the disposal of large numbers of eggs from the hatcheries on the town's outskirts when children found many live chicks hatching out where they had been dumped at Marley.

Some people in the town were too irresponsible to keep children let alone a dog the NSPCC Inspector, Mr Coleman, would say, for that was another side well-hidden which kept his department very busy which took the pressure off the police a bit but sometimes required the intervention of the police women when they really came into their own dealing with child neglect, rape and indecent assaults.

The police women's department in Keighley was headed by Sgt Margaret Carter, a stalwart of many years' service. With her slightly long navy-blue uniform skirt she reminded me of police women from the time of the Suffragettes. Margaret was a kind, motherly figure to us probationers of both sexes. Most of us were in our early twenties or in the case of the police women, late teens.

The four or so young police women we had in Keighley at any one time were quite beautiful, smart, above average intelligence and like all females for many of my generation, on a pedestal of respect. They were knowledgeable and well-spoken and in the eyes of some, capable of better things than the police.

In those times they worked a seven hour shift with an hour's break; they did not take part in regular patrols. Men worked an eight hour shift with a three-quarter of an hour break and had to parade fifteen minutes before the shift started

Being so attractive many of these young women were soon married and lost to the service. When, with equal rights they were incorporated into the general running of the police with the same duties as men I thought it a mistake. It seemed more appropriate to have some sort of a matron service by trained female staff retained and well-paid for those occasions when such were necessary involving bereavement, and offences concerning women and children.

I had seen young women attacked, knocked down by out-of- control violent men then kicked in the groin, screaming for help until the arrival of policeman and that was only at a common domestic dispute. It still seems repugnant to me to imagine some of the tasks they now have to do in the police and the armed forces. It is easy to brutalise someone but not so easy to redeem them from it and for someone as old-fashioned as me, I preferred the ladies to remain on that pedestal; after all there are plenty of men out there capable of doing the 'dirty dangerous work'!

There were two very special woman police officers who were in Road Traffic in the Keighley Division- Gill and Mary. They worked for years as a team and were liked by everyone, even the traffic offenders they reported who invariably thanked them for the warning or more seriously the report for summons. They had all the right qualities and were good company when they called at Keighley police station for their break. They never knew but we referred to them, kindly, as Gert and Daisy after a duo on the wireless.

The 1st Battalion the Gordon Highlanders marching to the former SS barracks on arrival from Dover to maintain peace between East and West during the height of the Cold War.

Chapter 18

The Firing Squad

This little story came from the mining district of the West Riding. It has a ring of truth about it and one could imagine it being very effective in preventing crime, albeit a little extreme for some.

Every police area in the country has persistent offenders who cause great upset and anger to the public. Such was the case with one Ivan, a refugee from Eastern Europe. His forte was stealing cars, any cars, working people's cars or rich people's cars. He was constantly before the courts who had tried various custodial sentences for juveniles but to no avail. He was now a man and still at it.

The sergeant in charge of the section was married to a miner's daughter and when her father's car was stolen her father was furious saying it was time the police got tough with Ivan. Pressure mounted on all the local police so they decided on a solution which was kept very secret. With only a few men in the know the sergeant started preparing for when Ivan was brought in again.

They didn't have to wait long. He'd stolen the Jaguar of the Worshipful Master of the local Lodge. There was uproar and once again there was pressure on the police to act so act they did.

Ivan, cocky as ever, was marched to the bottom of the cell corridor. A four man squad had taken the rifles out of the cabinet in the Inspectors office. They were hand-picked ex- servicemen from such regiments as the Coldstream Guards, The Green Howards, The Duke of Wellingtons and the Scots Guards.

Ivan heard the order given out of sight in the office.

"Squad, squad shun, by the right, right wheel quick march!"

The sound of rhythmic heavy soles heralded the smartest firing squad ever assembled since the Great War. Ivan stood to face them amazed. The sergeant went quickly to him.

"Do you wish to be blind folded?" he asked seriously.

Meanwhile the squad waited their rifles at the port. The sergeant stepped away from the prisoner and stood behind the squad. He was now holding a revolver, traditionally for the coup de grace.

"Squad, load, aim, fire!"

There was a deathly silence. A pool of water covered the tiled floor beneath Ivan who was shaking like a leaf.

"Squad, about turn; to your duties quick march!" ordered the sergeant.

They were gone as quickly as they had appeared and hopefully that would be the one and only such parade they would take part in.

The sergeant took two chairs to where Ivan was still standing and another officer brought two mug of tea. Indicating to Ivan to sit down he also sat beside him and had a sip of tea.

"You see these medal ribbons," said the sergeant in a very quiet tone. I earned them for fighting fascism at a time when Russia and the Allies fought side by side. We had a great regard for your old leader Uncle Joe Stalin, then we learned he'd killed more of his own people than the Nazis. What I am trying to tell you Ivan is you are lucky to live in our country where it is reasonably peaceful and there is no one likely to put you up against a wall and shoot you. Do you understand me?"

Ivan nodded and averting his eyes said, "Yes Sir!"

The sergeant continued: "In your country you would definitely be shot for the way you are behaving so gret a grip of yourself and let's have no more of it."

Once again Ivan nodded.

"Now listen carefully: nothing happened here tonight but it is just a reminder to you and people like you that we all have our breaking point so far as patience is concerned. Stop being a pain and start doing some good; life is very short for all of us and no one gets away with anything whether we catch them or not. We will not warn you again. Now drink your tea, wipe up that puddle and get in your cell. I'll try and put in a good word for you in Court in the morning."

Ivan was a changed man and there was great relief in the community but the community didn't know the lengths their police force would go to give them that relief!

Chapter 19

A River's Tale

A young boy was missing and his pal of the same age who had been with him would give no explanation. There was a massive hue and cry with officers and volunteers searching every likely hiding place in and around the town. Eventually his pal said they had been down at the river and the search was concentrated down there. The child was clearly frightened by what had happened and unable to give a precise spot where they had played so we walked each side of the river.

The banks on my side were steep and dangerous for they dropped into very deep, dark water. It was a place I had often fished as a boy taking great care but its darkness and gloom made it out of bounds for swimming. We had a natural fear of it for one of my relatives had drowned in this same river whilst playing.

There had been rain higher up the dales making the water look even more sinister.

The search was going badly, if only there was a clue but there appeared to be nothing to connect the child had ever been there.

There was one particular sweeping bend with high muddy banks and something made me take another look! Halfway between the bank top and the river was a scuff mark.
I knew something or someone had been there but just one mark could have been made by a bird.

The underwater rescue team found the poor soul on that bend and P.C. H had the sad duty of dealing with the child's death.

The death of a child, any child is one of the saddest experiences any officer has to suffer and it can live with him a long time. Nothing could have been done in this case; such drownings of children are still far too common for there is much water in the West Riding and children are naturally drawn to it.

All police officers in the West Riding had to have a life-saving certificate. One constable I knew who couldn't swim well was given an ultimatums to pass the life-saving exam or leave. He left to go to Australia where they were not so fussy.

The swimming baths were just up the road from the police station so they were used quite regularly to keep in shape. They were on number two beat and whilst working that beat one night I found the door of the baths insecure and went in. It was pitch black but I could hear strange sounds on the floor all around me. Not wishing to show a light in case there was an intruder I stood still and waited. The sounds continued so I switched on my torch. The whole of the floor area was alive with big, black cockroaches. What a sight! I reached for the electric light switch and brought more light on the scene. Within minutes the vast army of creepy insects had fled to the drains in the tiled floor and disappeared below. I don't suppose many folk would know they lived there. Had it been so there might have been fewer swimmers!

Once again on night duty observations with another constable in the grotty infamous town market watching from Roper's doorway the pouring rain and trickling water going down the rat-infested drains, we saw a figure in a light coloured trench-coat go and stand in a doorway opposite us and light a cigarette. Curious, I left my companion and went over. It was the Chief Inspector from our own station. He seemed annoyed that I had disturbed him and told me in no uncertain terms to 'F...off!'

To be spoken to by a senior officer in language usually applied by the criminals caused his reputation to fall to the level of the drains where the long-tailed furry things lived but I kept my views to myself and said nothing. He seemed abashed on our next meeting but did not apologise or offer an explanation.

Within the hierarchy of the Division there were undercurrents and rivalries and occasionally blatant dislikes such as we never had in the regiment where mutual respect was apparent at all levels. I put this down in the Police to the striving to go up the greasy ladder of promotion and confined to too small a building or perhaps it was just their nature to be unpleasant due to mixing with the underworld in order to get convictions!

Not all senior officers were like that. Chief Inspector Dixon who replaced the aforementioned was a gentleman, a countryman and a former Captain in the Duke of Wellington's Regiment during the war, more like the breed I was used to. Harold Weaver, the former Riddlesden Bobbie, one time Royal Navy during the war was promoted Chief Inspector for Skipton and he too was a cut above some. Tom Haigh was promoted Chief Inspector and put in an important role of the newly created Crime Squad. These men had earned their promotions. Others alas continued to be promoted supposedly on merit or perhaps because no one sought the elevation!

I was on night duty in Hanover Street when P.C. Brian Berry a very efficient constable from Northern Ireland came across from his beat to tell me President Kennedy had been assassinated. We were both shaken by the news for we knew that man had probably averted World War in dealing firmly with the Russian leadership over the Cuban Crises.

My friend, a drummer in the Black Watch band in Washington at the time played with the pipes and drums at the funeral. He retired from the army as a major and would have made an ideal CID officer but was too short!

All through the fifties and sixties there hung over all of us the prospect of a nuclear war. The Cuban crises involving President Kennedy and Nikita Khrushchev reminded everyone how fragile world peace was. Every police station, even the small rural ones, had an early warning system to inform of a nuclear attack. The resident constable was supposed to unpack the siren, drag it outside and start winding to produce that sound of attack some of us remember from World War Two. The warning gave us four minutes and as it took longer than that to assemble the siren, technically we were all dead.

Each year we attended a refresher Civil Defence Course where we familiarised ourselves with the latest apparatus, dosimeters and measuring devices to anticipate casualties from ground zero. For some reason I was radioactive. The only explanation I could give was a secret room beneath my barrack block in Germany which had radiation warning signs on it. I still wonder for we knew we were expendable.

The other annual Civil Defence exercise was the mobile column where a quite large number of police and advisors travelled the countryside living under canvas assessing the evacuation of towns in the event of war. They generally lasted about ten days and those attending seemed to enjoy it.

At the single day session involving about twenty men when the instruction was over it generally led to storytelling. I remember one such where the whole lesson was taken up with tales of a particular officer who we will call Yens. He was a likeable, intelligent, well-educated chap, half Scottish the other half from the fiords. He was very talented musically too and played in a well-known band. He would put himself out for anyone and by his actions brought much fun and pleasure to many. That day, nearly every man present had a tale to tell about Yens. All were harmless and funny, never derogatory. In fact everyone seemed proud to have enjoyed his company. His Burns suppers were famous and quite the best south of the border.

I will mention a couple of his escapades. This occurred early in his service when he arrested a man who might have been in Colditz for he promptly escaped pursued by Yens fearful of losing his good reputation. The escapee climbed up some scaffolding on a high building. Undaunted, the constable went up after him. A crowd quickly gathered and the press were soon on the scene. Yens was considered by some to be something of a hero for 'rescuing' the prisoner. The sequel to the tale is he was required to attend Buckingham Palace where he was presented with a medal.

Another incident involved his music. Posted to guard the safety of the Road Traffic Building at night he locked himself in thinking he would be undisturbed until morning when he was ready to go off duty. Unfortunately, the Traffic Superintendent needed to get into the building urgently. Unable to get an answer to his telephone calls he asked for an officer to be sent round. This officer could not gain access for the door was locked but he could see lights on. He could also hear the penetrating sound of a trombone or Tuber or some such wind instrument repeatedly playing scales. He grinned to himself on his way back to the station but dreaded telling the Superintendent. Fortunately, tired of waiting, he'd gone and Yens had an uninterrupted shift playing Gilbert and Sullivan comic opera – so fitting!

Chapter 20

Transfer

From its historical centre in York the county of Yorkshire was divided into three from the earliest times – North Riding, East Riding and West Riding, riding meaning a third in the old language. It remained thus until the 70s when great confusion was caused and the loss of tribal identity when the boundaries were altered by people who seemingly did not understand the ancient ties. Also at that time the leaders took the country into the Common Market, another controversial and doubtful venture as history has shown. Those who lead will take the blame; those who follow will see their shame!

In 1964 the Ridings were still intact and I was transferred over the hill into Wharfedale to the village of Addingham. The Police house left much to be desired it being a Victorian terrace house in the Bolton Abbey Road with a West Riding caste metal sign over the door. The interior was painted in pre-war dark brown paint and the remnant of gas mantles were in each room plus the early warning system for nuclear attack just inside the door with the telephone. A black-leaded Yorkist range was the only heating. That I didn't mind for I had grown up with such.

The biggest shock was the tippler toilet in the back yard (there was no garden) and this operated when washing up water from the sink collected in a pan beneath the yard flagstones and tippled the water into the actual toilet. This was an eight foot long, one foot diameter pipe dropping down straight into the visible sewer. For comfort it was covered with rough, painted boards with a 10" hole. There was no sign of newspapers on the back of the door but this was from that era.

Woodworm infested every room and the bath stood alone and forlorn in a tiny room. How the weight of it hadn't caused the worm-eaten floor to collapse I don't know.

Looking through the cupboard next to the telephone there were orders and records going back to 1900.

As I locked the place up I was thinking it would be the last visit for resignation was crossing my mind. In that day and age surely the Great British Police Force should have something better to offer.

As we were driven back over Cringles I looked back with the sun on the beacon and the fresh colours of the spring leaves and the white May blossom and thought a house was not everything for it was truly a beautiful beat and I had been selected for it for a reason.

I spoke to the Chief Inspector in Skipton. He understood my feelings on the house but assured me a new house was to be built by the railway station at Bolton Abbey and that I would be the first to occupy it. I can't say I believed this would happen for I had heard similar promises when working for the aristocracy on large sporting estates.

However, we got busy scrubbing and brought workmen in to deal with the woodworm and other necessary repairs.

After three days of this I took my bagpipes and went for a walk by the river Wharfe which I had fished as a boy with my father and grandfather. I was on leave and no one yet knew I was the new policeman.

Music, whether playing or listening is wonderful for restoring flagging energy, especially the pipes once outlawed by the British Government because they incited men to brave deeds!

It was late evening, the light was failing and ducks were flying along with an old heron going to roost. No one else was there and for a few moments I had escaped from painting and decorating then I heard a voice above the tune I was playing. I continued until the end of the measure then stopped abruptly, as pipers do.

A little man in a flat cap, jacket and waistcoat stood before me

"There's no footpath along the river; you shouldn't be down here," he said in a very unfriendly tone.

I had no wish to argue with the man but felt I had to say something because I knew what he said could not be right.

"I walked this path during and after the war with my grandfather and my father when he returned. They had always walked it."

"Then they'd no right to," he said "I'll walk you to the gate."

We walked in silence, my pleasant evening brought to an abrupt end with this disagreeable person. It was now fairly dark and on arrival at the road I noticed the farmer's car was parked in a dangerous position on the wrong side of the road without lights. I was never vindictive but I confess for a moment it was tempting to report him for the offences he was committing but I left him to it and returned to my decorating. Enquiring from my milkman George Atkins next day he advised me to have words with Madge Adams in High Mill Lane near the footpath.

"She walks it every day," said George "Takes a chair with her to climb over the barbed wire. The villagers have always used the footpath and Madge is in her 70s and feels very strongly about it!" This sounded as though it could lead to trouble in this small community and how right I was but for the moment house cleaning was more important.

The following morning I cleaned the toilet box and seat and painted it green. It looked much better but really it was out of the Ark. It must have been the last one left in the valley. Even my neighbours had flush toilets, outside of course!

Harry, my police pal and his wife came over from Keighley to lend a hand. I thought to show him round the village and when we came back I was in trouble.

My wife was irate, "Why didn't you leave a sign saying the paint was wet in the loo?" she asked.

She was speaking from the kitchen and through the half-open door I caught a glimpse of Harry's wife with her dress held high and my wife doing her best to erase the large green circle of paint. Of course we did nothing but laugh and in time they saw the funny side of it. One little girl who visited told her mum we had "a make believe loo." I put a report in straight away for a modern flush toilet.

Officially I was still on leave but a neighbour asked to speak to me about his brother-in-law who ran a business on his land which he wanted to terminate. I was with him some time gaining local knowledge and explaining it was a civil matter and his solicitor would advise him. I was getting the feeling there was much dissent among the people. This man was quite helpful warning me that the main Addingham families were all related and that to upset one was to upset them all. I promised to bear that in mind.

Returning to the police house I found Big Harry jubilant. He'd been looking over the wall into the beck when he saw a rat feeding on food a neighbour had thrown out. In my absence he amused himself sitting on the wall shooting them with my gun. In all he shot twelve. There was no more feeding ducks over the wall after that.

Exchanging my highland dear forest on Royal Deeside for the Yorkshire Wharfedale beat.

Chapter 21

The Rural Beat

The beat comprised Addingham, Draughton and Bolton Abbey. Bolton Abbey had been a separate beat until recent times but there was no longer any suitable accommodation there for a single man. Three officers now worked the two beats – Norman Lister who lived in the Police house with the office alongside and Bob Copeland who lived in digs and now myself.

Norman was an amiable chap who had served in the Royal Air Force during the war; Bob had done his National Service with the Royal Navy. Norman introduced me to the shopkeepers and as many locals as possible.

There were five weaving sheds still working, five public houses, one British Legion Club and one off licence; three butchers shops, two iron mongers and one fish and chip shop. There was a Coop near my house which supplied groceries and animal feed stuffs to the farmers; three part time banks, Dr Wynn's surgery, Eddie Blagborough's coal business, a Station Master Austin Burdock for we still had the railway; and four milkmen, Freddie Blaythorne, Mr. Snowden, Mr. Wallbank and George Atkins all selling milk produced locally. The most useful to the farming community was Billie Brear's saw Mill.

Religion was well catered for with a Roman Catholic Church, an Anglican church and two Methodist churches, one more primitive than the other! The school was Methodist controlled standing near to where John Wesley preached.

I met many people that day; some I would remember, some I wouldn't. All were friendly, especially the five licensees which was to be expected as most of the problems in society could be traced back to alcohol. At least, that's how it seemed to most police officers which was why licensed premises were so controlled and subject to inspection by the police.

The following day I was on my own, walking the beat in uniform. My points were every hour at ten to the clock and we were expected to be at the appointed telephone kiosk five minutes before and five minutes after.

Everyone I met spoke and were very friendly quite different from the town over the hill. I gleaned little snippets of information; saw a few cars out of Bolton Road the junction being blind due to the Crown building on one side and Martins Bank on the other. It was worse at weekends with the returning Bolton Abbey traffic. Without a constable there to help it really was on a wing and a prayer for Main Street was the A65 Trunk road, notorious for accidents.

Passing the Fleece Hotel at lunchtime a figure lurched out of the door. He wore a flat cap, was unshaven and his jacket was full of holes. I took him for a gentleman of the road and asked him where he had slept the night. He looked at me with a puzzled expression and said, "At 'ome, where do you think?"

"And where's home?" I asked in all innocence.

"I'nt' Manor House of course," he gruffly replied.

I back peddled quickly hoping he hadn't twigged what I had been thinking.

"It's Mr Brear from the saw mill," I said "You were in Harris tweeds when last I saw you. I really didn't recognise you in your working clothes."

He grinned and said, "Come in for a pint" and he knew exactly what I had been thinking!

I explained that I did not drink alcohol.

"Then come and have a cup of tea with us when you're passing."

I thanked him and promised to do that.

It transpired that Lilian, his wife, was the finest sponge cake maker in the village.

"Incidentally," I asked, "Who owns that field behind the Bolton Road Police house   because it's alive with rats?"

"It's A W" he replied.

And who owns the field down by the river near High Mill?"

"That's him as well."

"Are you both on the Parish Council?"

Billie nodded and left me at Jimmy Hadley's garage where the sign said 'Free petrol tomorrow'

Jimmy saw me coming and left his man, Freddie Metcalfe to carry on mending a car. Discovering I didn't have a car of my own he tried to sell me one. In his office he had photographs of all the men from Addingham who went off to the war including those who did not return. He was very much involved with the Parish Council, the Memorial Hall and the concerts that were put on there. He came to Addingham from Thwaites, Keighley, and had his house built on Bark Lane by the Ridley brothers with local stone from Addingham's communal quarry up the Roman Road.. It was a fine house. All Addingham residents had a right to take stone from that quarry but in the 70s when Bradford took over, they used it as a refuse tip, filled it in and obliterated it and the village lost another ancient rite and a habitat for meadow pipits, skylarks and wagtails.

After lunch at my home station I set off to walk to Draughton dodging the heavy goods vehicles and walking on the grass verge where possible. At Chelker reservoir I watched a pair of great crested grebes and a pair of Bean geese. They were unusual and these were the first I had seen in England. There were lots of tufted ducks but not a single angler fishing. What a waste I thought. There would be many a working man would like to fish that water but I learned it belonged an exclusive club and it was 'dead men's shoes' to get in.

During the course of my walk I was observed by the Skipton Superintendent who left a message for me to get a bike as he thought I might get run over! He obviously did not think to give me a lift in his car but I took his advice and got me a Sunbeam from P.C. Allinson. It wasn't too bad going down hills but the gears had seen better days and going uphill was torture with the risk of serious injury in the groin when the gears crashed. I rarely used the bike and eventually gave it to P.C. Jeffrey.

At Draughton post office I made my point at the kiosk and was startled to hear it ring. The message was for me and there was a confirmed case of Anthrax at Mr. Lomas's in Draughton. It was a beautiful Jersey cow that lay dead outside his barn down Cow Mucker Lane and he was very upset for she gave good milk. We dragged her onto open ground and awaited the burners coming from Skipton. One of my extra duties was as Diseases of Animals Inspector.

Anthrax was a deadly disease which we suspected came in the animal feed from South America where it was common and as bone-meal was used in the feed we suspected that was how it came across. I heard of a gardener dying after pricking himself on a rose after feeding plants with bone meal. One couldn't be too careful. There was no cure at that time.

A message was sent to my home station to inform my wife I was tied up and would not be home for tea.

During the war one of the Hebridean Islands was sown with anthrax as an experiment with a view to using the disease against our enemies but it didn't happen. In the 60s the island was still out of bounds for fear of contamination.

Sergeant Abbot arrived with cans of disinfectant and wellington boots followed by an expert with the burners. The burning of a cow takes a long time even with modern oxyacetylene burners but a great improvement on the old-fashioned method of coal and timber after digging a huge pit which we formerly used.

The sergeant departed leaving me with the farmer and the man to control the two burners. The constable had to be there to ensure it was done hygienically and thoroughly. Fortunately it was fine but it took from mid-afternoon until eleven o'clock at night to complete the job.

We stunk of burning flesh and singing hair and were desperate for a bath. My uniform would go to the cleaners but it was a day or two before the smell had left the nostrils. Thank goodness Anthrax didn't strike too often. In all I dealt with three actual cases and many false alarms.

What I quickly learned was the value of the intelligence network between the people in the villages and the police. If a 'strange person' appeared it was not long before we heard about it and folks were quick to become involved and help at accidents and even in 'rough houses' usually caused by girls or drink at the public houses. The advantage of this was the prevention of crime of all kinds and at times it was amazing what turned up from an innocent remark of a suspicious local. Still living in the village it is noticeable how all that goodwill has been lost which would be invaluable now when the country faces the threat of terrorism again!

Chapter 22

Corned beef and Oranges

Road accidents were a regular occurrence and officers always carried two large triangular bandages in the inside pocket of the tunic plus a tape measure for measuring fatal casualties. The Addingham trunk road to Skipton and the Skipton to Harrogate trunk road were hilly with notorious bends where many vehicles came to grief.

The blind bend in Draughton was constantly getting blocked when two heavy wagons met. One such was a truck laden with 7lb tins off corned beef. It caused chaos for there were tins whole and squashed all over the road, pavement and grass verge. Draughtonites, remembering the war, were not prone to wasting anything and whilst the driver was in the kiosk ringing his boss and before I arrived on the scene, they were clearing up the mess, but only the whole, undamaged tins.

By the time I got a lift and began interviewing the two drivers there was quite a crowd. They had that air about them like school children who have done something or are about to do something naughty.

Having cleared one vehicle away and got the traffic moving there was now the problem of the corned beef's security and the clearing up of the masses of damaged tins. The driver was instructed to return to his base and leave the clear-up until the next day. I pointed out the Police would only be able to make spot visits to the site to which he said, "Well, they'll all be honest Methodists out here, won't they." I already had my doubts about that and by next day I was certain!

Talk about picking the bones clean. Not a single tin was left that was any good and I reasoned that every house in the village would be eating corned beef for days. Had I gone poking about in the dustbins the evidence of the empty tins would have been staring me in the face and I would have been obliged to say something but I didn't for a similar accident on the Skipton Road near to Halton East demanded my attention.

A lorry carrying a load of boxed Savile oranges had failed to take the bend near Draughton Road end shedding its load. There were boxes of oranges in the fields, on top of the walls, in the hedge and all over the verges ripe juicy fruit there for the taking. The only difference with the corned beef bonanza this latest 'jackpot' was out in the countryside some way from habitation.

Having taken details from the driver I discussed security of the cargo. "Don't tell anyone," he said, "But the boss doesn't really care; it will be an insurance claim." I reminded him he could well be prosecuted for driving without due care and attention. "It's a daily hazard," he said "These roads are not really suitable for heavy vehicles; they were built for horse and carts." I agreed.

Skipton Road Traffic patrols were asked to pay attention to the crash site when they could but they covered a vast area from Sedbergh to Ilkley and I didn't anticipate much supervision there.

I returned to the scene early the following day. The first thing I noticed was a footpath where no footpath had been leading all the way to the hamlet of Halton East. The Saville oranges had gone and I could imagine the locals trundling up the steep field, boxes on their backs like Cornish ship wreakers of old having looted a ship. It was a bit similar and despite it being theft they would be horrified to think so. So it was that the W.I. had a glut of quality marmalade to sell at their functions and the locals couldn't wait for the next gift horse!

A lorry carrying tons of salt overturned on the Sailor bend in Addingham. Word soon got round and Johnny Walker, a gentleman farmer, appeared and offered to remove the salt if he could have it. The driver was lying with a makeshift splint waiting for the ambulance but he gave Johnny his firms details. To Johnny's delight the firm agreed and as soon as the lorry was removed his man George set to with a shovel filling load after load of the tractor's trailer. I asked Johnny what he would do with the salt.

"Spread it on t'land," he said with glee, "spread it on t'land!"

Johnny or Pop as we used to call him had been a special sergeant during the war when the black market was rife. He made regular trips to the York area returning at night. After one of these mysterious outings the Home Guard stopped his car at Sand beds. Of course they all knew him and one jokingly said,

"Have you got a few hams under t'seat Johnny lad?"

"Nay lad, you know me better than that," said Johnny chuckling as he drove away. Not only were there hams there was even a goat he'd bought for ten shillings which his man George skinned out and draped a bit of lamb's fat round its kidneys. Johnny inspected the freshly killed lambs and the goat before they were taken to Ilkley market wondering who the lucky person would be eating 'old Billie'" for the goat was not young.

One night Pop rang up to say their house had been burgled. Entry was by breaking a downstairs window. It seemed food was the main thing stolen plus two of Pop's brand new suits. Mrs. Walker was very upset talking only of moving house. I reassured her that we would catch the thieves for I had an inkling two were involved.

On the arrival of their son John we went to look in a barn a short distance from the house.

"Was that ladder up to the hay-loft?" I asked John.

"No, definitely not," he replied.

Taking him outside I asked him to stand by the door whilst I climbed the ladder and if I should ask for the dogs to be released to say "Right!" We had no dogs nor did I ask him to bark like one though it crossed my mind.

I climbed the ladder and shone my torch into the hay. Sure enough, the burglars were there, fast asleep on top of Pop's new suits. It was an abrupt awakening but they came quietly. Once we were down the ladder I handcuffed them together.

Because Mrs Walker was so upset I felt it necessary to let her see the sort of people who would enter her home. They were two 17 year old youths on the run from an Approved School and certainly not worth leaving home for. They were duly returned.

Pop liked nothing better than to get one over on someone like himself. His brother Abe was similar. It was Abe who had got into difficulties by trying to close the river footpath, a long-established path which became part of the National Dales Way. This battle led to his house being tarred and feathered, two barns being burned down, his tires slashed and a row of trees he had planted to hide the 'peasants' houses, cut down. He no long sat on the Parish Council.

When they passed away I guided both their hearses out from their homes for they were bad exits and I can think of nothing worse than a lorry running into a funeral cortege!

Sometimes I tried to imagine how it would be without a police force; that we were interfering with the natural scheme of things by protecting everyone under the law. I suppose without us it would be a smaller population, fewer vehicles, fewer prisons and fewer prisoners for the 'good guys' would see off the bad guys! If only it were so simple!

What I am so certain of is that no one escapes from their wrongdoing. It really matters not that the police cannot bring offenders to justice they always get their comeuppance one way or another, or at least from what I have seen it keeps me on the straight and narrow! I wish it did with the rest of them then what a world we'd have!

Chapter 23

Never, ever let your gun pointed be at anyone

Once the shooting season began in August to February a visitor to Wharfedale could be forgiven for believing he was in the Middle East or the Balkans. From every direction there came gunshots even on the Sabbath which used to be sacred when no self-respecting gamekeeper would be seen to carry a gun.

Control of all firearms since the war had been lax. As boys we all had them and all that was required for a shotgun was a ten shilling licence from the post office. For a rifle or a revolver it was a little more involved but just as cheap. For a time no fee at all was required for a shotgun.

Of course the farmers, gamekeepers and landowners did not like all this irregular, unauthorised shooting and made complaints. They knew of my background as a naturalist and former keeper and expected me to act. I caught a few groups of young men. If they had not shot anything I made them promise not to come again or they would be prosecuted. They seemed happy with that but for me it nearly proved fatal.

Two weeks after cautioning two lads with a Canadian, single-barrelled shotgun who had just got onto private land but had shot nothing I heard shooting from the railway line. We still had trains at that time and there was plenty of cover for game such as pheasants, partridge's hares and rabbits. Slipping on an old jacket over my uniform I walked along the side of the track.

There followed a chase of a man with a gun across the railway line into the park at Farfield. He was determined to get away from me but I was gradually gaining and when just thirty feet from him he stopped abruptly, put the gun up to his shoulder and pointed it straight at me.

I identified myself and asked him to put the gun down saying that if he shot me he would go to prison for life and no man should go to prison for poaching game. He hesitated, weighing up the consequences but then he placed the gun on the ground. I picked it up and took out the cartridge recognising the gun as one in possession of two lads a fortnight before when I had cautioned them and let them go.

I reported him for a variety of game-related offences but not for pointing the gun. I told him he was a very stupid man that he would probably get 14 years just for pointing the gun at me if I prosecuted him for that. He nodded but said nothing.

Here was another dilemma having been brought up always to turn the other cheek. I could leave it for the lawyers and the Judge at the Assize court or forgive and forget now. The pursuit of wild game has always been an attraction for country lads, me included, and I could understand him. Raising the gun was definitely not acceptable but I would not like to see his life ruined because of a brief, chance encounter in a field. I told him he would be prosecuted for the poaching offences at Skipton. I had already taken possession of the gun and cartridges. If he had shot anything he had disposed of it on seeing me.

Some weeks later he appeared at Skipton Court. He told me he was pleading not guilty to the poaching offences because I had let two lads off previously with the same gun.

In that case, I said," I'll have to charge you with pointing the gun at me for such an offence is never cancelled until it is brought before the Assize court. It may be a long sentence. I've been more than fair with you but this is your last chance. If you plead not guilty I will arrest you now and have you remanded in custody. The charge may be attempted murder!".

The chap pleaded guilty and was fined a few pounds.

Some men just cannot understand when even a copper is doing them a kindness and this copper learned yet again that leniency is not always prudent

The English game laws were enacted from 1829, 1830 and 1831 coinciding with the invention of the breach-loading gun. Thereafter, the landed gentry, mostly members of the Whig or Liberal party, started to rear game on a large scale to provide for shooting parties at the stately homes therefore country people who had always subsidised their meagre food rations with the odd rabbit or pheasant found themselves seriously outside the law. Daytime poaching was bad enough but night poaching meant trial at the Assize. Prison and deportation to the colonies was common.

Ralph Waldo Emerson, the American writer said 'The English Game Laws are the most oppressive acts perpetrated against a free people'.

Even my generation accepted that a wild creature belonged to the person who could catch it and according to scripture 'The Earth is the Lord's and the Fullness thereof' in other words no one can really own land, it belongs to everyone. Some people would charge us for breathing the air over their property. I don't think it was ever intended to be like this. Them and us has always led to division, revolution and war but this is the World and this is how it is for now and if those put in authority cannot use a bit of common sense and dish out a bit of leniency now and again we really have slipped down on the scale.

The Prime Minister Sir Harold McMillan was a regular member of the Duke of Devonshire's grouse shooting party at Bolton Abbey and on this occasion the grouse came so thick and fast that he accidently shot and killed a kestrel, a protected bird. Turning to his protection officer he reputedly said, "Sergeant, you will have to arrest me; I've just shot a kestrel."

Mr. E H, the Duke's agent for the estate, also shot regularly. Now shooting can be a dangerous thing not just from the gun but the birds themselves. Mr. H shot and killed a grouse which was travelling at a mighty speed. The bird struck him hard in the chest causing great pain and absence from his duties for a while.

In the forces I had been a marksman with the rifle but now I was a revolver shot because of the political situation. My duties included examining all firearms held in my area. Visiting Mr. H was always a pleasure for he had some interesting stories to tell. He had served as agent on an estate in Ireland when the Land League were trying to bring improvements to the tenants, often of absentee landlords, which led to violent disputes and Mr H had to return to England at short notice.

Officially, his revolver was for shooting rogue deer. I pointed out that the red deer herd had been shot out for food during the 1930s depression and that I had only then started seeing the odd roe deer. He laughed because he knew of my pedigree, of my knowledge of Irish history and the Michael Davitt Land League. Indeed he was still good friends with local landowners originally from Ballina, Co. Mayo, where some of my forebears came from. It was nice to see such people rise up in the world!

Many times I tried to persuade him to reintroduce red deer to the estate but he would not saying, they would be a nuisance to the farmers. I am sure he was right yet the circular feeding station for the deer up at the Deer Park through which one passed on the way to Simon's Seat was still visible on snowy days. I first thought this stone circle to be an ancient British site but he explained it was a feed trap for selecting which deer to kill for food!

Chapter 24

The Streak

Addingham cricketers were a proud and devoted breed of players with a good following of old and young who would congregate each weekend to sit and watch the game. Two of the regulars were Mr Hargreaves and Mr W Flesher now into their eighties. They sat by the dry stone wall putting the world to right whilst keeping an eye on the players. There was not a great deal of excitement in their lives now but that hadn't always been the case. Part of Kitchener's Army of Old Contemptibles, they had fought in the trenches in France and Belgium in the Great War and each had been wounded but at least they came back unlike so many whose names were on the War Memorial.

Cricket is one of those games that assure you all is well with our country. To see the white clad figures dotted about the green is not unlike Drake playing bowls when the Spanish Invasion fleet was growling at the door for always there is danger and unrest and yet the game of cricket and football goes on.

The day was warm and as often was the case the two old gentlemen dozed off for a while content with their little world. Clapping was the norm when the game produced a success but never shouting and cheering. It was the latter that awoke Mr.Flesher who had lost his arm at Passiondaele, had been a moorland gamekeeper and was more alert than some. He scanned the field through half-closed eyes which nearly popped out of his head. Nudging his companion he said,

"Mr Hewadine am I mistaken or is that a young woman running round the pitch without her clothes.

Now fully awake Mr. Hewadine shielded his eyes in excitement and searched the field perimeter.

"Eh, your reight," he burst out, "It's a wench in the nude and she's coming this way; by gum but she's a beauty with that blonde hair; just like Lady Godiva!"

Totally absorbed in the spectacle which they found hard to believe they watched and waited as the young lady passed close by. She fairly bounced along and as she reached the pavilion a great roar of applause went up from the other spectators and players.

Turning to Mr. Flesher, Mr Hewadine said, "She's as bonnie from t'rear as she is from front, just like those French lasses were in Picardy."

It was time for a cup of tea and the happy pair ambled to the pavilion where they listened to the team captain thanking Beth, the gem of Addingham's Crown for responding to a wager and daring to carry out the streak. She was from a good local family and some thought her actions had resulted in an Addingham win against Silsden.

Thereafter the numbers of spectators attending the cricket matches doubled for a while but there was no repeat performance. The two old soldiers couldn't wait to tell me as they walked up to the Fleece but they weren't complaining. The sixteen year old girl had made their day whatever the new Rector might think about it. Those who were there saw it as a harmless prank, a repeat of a similar streak at Lords cricket ground by a male. The difference being he was arrested. There would be no arresting the Gem of Addingham's Crown!

The Methodist Church members caused a few raised eyebrows when a number of them changed partners, apparently quite amicably, to the consternation of some of the Anglicans. It was really nothing to do with anybody; a private natural happening for that time of the year. After the things I had seen in the village I raised no eyebrows and the secrets I had will never be revealed. However, we had got a new Rector in the Anglican Church. Some people like a bit of publicity and by heaven we got that.

Warm weather does cause people to take their clothes off and so it was down at the river with a group of young people having a midnight bathe. They were all sons and daughters of old Addingham families doing what their forebears had done down the years. It was harmless, healthy and perfectly natural. Sadly not everyone thought so and the Rector was informed and for some reason the village found its name tarnished in the News of the World and labelled 'Sin City' for it was coupled with a few other goings on. This was found amusing by some and resented by others. As Mrs B said, "Vicars practising in the Yorkshire Dales should be local, Northern men who understood the customs and ways of the people; one couldn't expect people from the midlands or further south to have a clue" She was probably right but Mrs B could be very outspoken! However, the unnecessary publicity gave the village a poor reputation but time wears all away.

Cricket pavilions have always been an attraction for young people to congregate for a secret bottle of ale, a fag or to play games.

The view from the police office gave a good view of the field adjoining the cricket field and when I saw a stream of local youths of all ages using the field to enter the pavilion from the rear I was curious. They had that slinky, give-away look as if they were about to do something they shouldn't so I thought I'd take a look later on.

They were on the veranda busy with a game of something. Walking up quite openly in cape and helmet to give them a chance to run away if they wished I got nearer and nearer. They were totally engrossed like little old men and they never knew I was there until I stood alongside looking down on their card game. A pile of money was on the table so it looked serious. One looked up, saw me and nearly fainted.

"Stay where you are and leave everything as it is," said I. They obliged but looked very sheepish. Well, they were hardly the Les Vegas professionals!

I knew them all but took down their names and addresses etc. to make it look more official, took possession of the cards and money and told them I would see them with their parents over the next few days explaining that gambling in a public place was an offence. As I escorted them back to the village they were subdued but respectful and polite when we went our different ways.

"Do you think he'll book us?" I heard one of the younger ones ask.

"He might," said master Rishworth, "We'll have to wait and see."

Now one may think that a bit of unlawful gambling would have no connection to other matters in the village except it required money to play. One young man in the game had already been interviewed by my colleague regarding some burglaries where money was taken to no avail.

I asked his father to bring him down to the office and there I asked a few questions of the boy who was clearly hiding something. His dad was well known to me and eager to get to the bottom of this as the householders were. I asked him to wait in the garden for a few minutes. Without his father present the boy spilled the beans. Yes, he'd taken the money to play cards with the big boys.

Dealing with juveniles was always a bit tricky when they were suspects. Sometimes parents could be hostile to the police and that could make matters worse. Most village Bobbies went to great lengths to save young people from gaining a criminal record but sometimes parents made that impossible and mistaken loyalties led to their child getting into further trouble. With the odd exception the local police had a first class relationship with parents and matters were dealt with quietly without fuss or juvenile court appearances. Very few were prosecuted.

In the case of the youthful gamblers no action was taken, the money etc. was handed to a parent and shared out with the culprits who were quite numerous. Addingham may have been labelled Sin City but we didn't want everyone to have a court experience!

Headingley cricket ground is the famous headquarters of the Yorkshire County team and one day I received information that the large safe had been stolen from the office there and might be hidden at a certain farm. It wasn't difficult to find stuck out at the back of the farmhouse covered over with timber. The two culprits were arrested by CID in Leeds but they asked me to arrange collection of the safe. I dealt directly with Headingley and they arranged for a large truck from Pickford's to collect it.

How the thieves managed to steal it let alone get it to the isolated farm we never knew but when I heard of how the removal men fared taking their huge truck up the narrow lane to shift such a weight I was glad I was not there. Perhaps it contained gold for it was still unopened and the contents intact.

Chapter 25

Slightly Unorthodox

A police officer had been murdered down south and there was a hue and cry to try and catch the criminal. As often happens in such serious cases the publicity leads to false sightings all over the country. The villain was known to have survival skills, the ability to live off the land.

The section sergeant from Silsden informed me there had been a sighting of a suspicious man in the rock caves on the Addingham Moorside ridge. As the man was armed it would have meant waiting for over an hour for a firearms officer to arrive from Wakefield. I pointed out I had firearms and was well-versed in their use being a marksman with the rifle. I suggested we put on civvies jackets and went rabbit shooting without troubling Wakefield. I had written authority to shoot rabbits anyway so we didn't need to involve anyone else. In any case we both knew it would be a false alarm with good intent.

The sergeant was a heavy man and the terrain was hard going but he survived the exercise and when we had completed a thorough search agreed it had been a sensible idea although he was just a bit windy at first. I had been a trained revolver shot for some time but preferred the rifle. Sergeant Abbott was a decent, fair man. Like so many supervisory officers he had served in the forces during the war. I noted that promotion meant more and more sedentary work, hardly conducive to fitness and good health.

The suspect was eventually caught living in the forest in his own territory as we knew he would be.

To ensure police from the outlying districts were maintaining high standards of behaviour and fitness and to remind them they belonged to a large, powerful organisation and because most worked in remote places in isolation, drill parades were held once a month in the army drill hall in Skipton.

Perhaps sixty or more men would be called in from their often remote, isolated beats dressed in best uniform with boots highly polished. There was still much of the military discipline about the police force at this time which held things together and got things done without argument. Like the armed forces, it was the only way the system could work properly for the benefit of the public, though some would disagree.

What happened on this particular parade was not typical but it was memorable for all who attended. The routine was for the men to line up in three ranks at open order to be inspected by the Superintendent accompanied by the training officer from headquarters in Wakefield. This officer had served in the guards and was very regimental. He accompanied the superintendent along the ranks looking for reasons to comment on individual turnout. At one officer he noticed he was wearing the General Service Medal and asked him where he'd served.

"Cyprus," replied the constable in a broad Scottish accent.

"What were you in?" asked the ex-guardsman.

"The Gordon Highlanders, Sir," replied the constable.

Now the ex-guardsman carried a polished stick and when referring to the constable's medal he had poked him with the stick in the chest. What happened next was a poke too far.

The ex-guardsman leant close to the former Gordon Highlander and said,

"I was in Cyprus; you were a bad lot," and poked the constable in the chest again.

The whole parade had heard the remarks and one could have heard a pin drop. The Gordon coloured up and still holding the position of attention said in finest Doric accent:

"If you f...ingwell poke me again with that f...ing stick I'll break it over your scraggy neck and shove it down your f...ing throat.

The Drill Instructor coughed but said not a word, continuing down the line of men. There was no chuckling from the ranks but there were definitely a few grins for this was soldier's talk and well justified. Technically the ex-Gordon had been assaulted by the poke from the stick and that could have been very embarrassing for the drill instructor had a complaint been made.

Churchill said of the Gordon Highlanders: 'The Finest Regiment in the World!' And he should know for he had seen them in action and knew them well. As regards Cyprus sixteen Gordon Highlanders were killed in Cyprus, seven in a single day; others shot in the back by terrorists or freedom fighters as they would have seen themselves; over four hundred British Servicemen died and over twenty police officers were murdered during the emergency of the 50s. To have anyone speak ill of one's regiment, especially a Scottish regiment is asking for trouble.

This light-entertainment gave us something to chat about over a cup of tea in Skipton. Presumably the embarrassment was settled amicably in the end but was it the reason for Drill Parades to be discontinued which they were soon after?

Among the army of blue uniforms defending what was right against what was wrong was a sprinkling of what can only be called characters. One such came to the village after what we saw as a humorous transgression but his Superintendent did not, therefore he was banished to the dales from south of the county.

Most officers were on foot with a few on bicycles then an experiment was carried out with a handful of Ford Popular cars on selected beats. These vehicles were painted black indistinguishable from any other Ford but for the bolted on Police sign on the roof. When Mo drove his new beat car back from Wakefield he was ecstatic and his mind was full of possibilities for to own a car was out of the question for most constables with families, life being difficult enough.

Mo had gained his driving licence in the military and he was an experienced traveller but his wife and children were not. His coming rest day fell on a weekend and he thought to give the family the treat of a lifetime. They would go to the seaside. The police sign was easily removed and with buckets and spades they set off for Blackpool. The children had only ever heard of it and were very excited at the prospect of the tower and the sea which they had never seen. Parking the car safely the happy family played on the sands, paddled in the sea and rode on the donkeys. The sea air was giving them an appetite so it was fish and chips for lunch then a ride on the ghost train.

It was on their way to Stanley Park to see the gold fish that constable Mo received his first pangs of anxiety. As they drove up the promenade he thought he recognised the car coming towards him.

"Get down!" he shouted to his brood but they were too excited and misunderstood.

"What is it?" asked his puzzled wife..

"That was the Superintendent's car," said Mo with some alarm

"Well, he might not have seen us," said Mrs Mo.

"Oh but he did; I saw the expression on his face and he'd recognise the WR of the West Riding number plate. Now I'm for it."

"Don't worry love, we've had a grand day out and surely you've earned that with all the time you put in for which you're never paid a penny.

"Anyway, here's Stanley Park said Mo; it's no use worrying now."

The constable's punishment for improper use of a police vehicle was his transfer to the dales. It might have been more severe but the police car was a novelty for a beat man and police pay was very little with long hours of duty with no overtime pay!

Once he'd settled in, Mo was on duty at Bolton Abbey. It was Sunday morning and he'd bought a paper. As it was quiet he thought he would have a smoke and a read for it was a fine sunny day and there was time between his point at the post office. Climbing through the hedge he found a sunny bank, removed his tunic and lay back, his glasses balanced on his nose end. The birds were singing, traffic and visitors were light and life was very good away from the wife and brood. Mo dozed off to sleep and missed his point which led to Sergeant Abbott driving out to find him with details from Skipton of a missing person believed heading for the Strid.

The sergeant knew the constable very well and it didn't take very long to find him, giving him a dressing down on the spot and pointing out what a disgrace if the Duke or Duchess had seen him. He apologised but knew not to give any undertaking that it wouldn't happen again!

Chapter 26

The right place at the right time

From foot patrol to the pedal cycle to the Noddy Bike or Velocette motor cycle, the West Riding slowly modernised resulting in more 'bad backs' for riding up hill and down dale in all weathers was not conducive to fitness and robust health. The motor bike was awkward if one had a prisoner to deal with but they did have a radio which really was invaluable when requiring assistance miles from anywhere at a road accident, for instance. They also had a pannier on each side which had their uses and they were very quiet runners.

However, when requiring to run in pursuit of some miscreant the machine had to be set up on its stand on level ground and the rider had first to cast off his gauntlets, helmet and heavy-duty coat for there was no hope in catching anyone in all that clobber. On occasion I have seen all that gear scattered across the field whilst in hot pursuit only to return with the prisoner to find the 'Noddy' had fallen off its stand and broken the windscreen. Trying to explain the damage would have meant endless paperwork but fortunately the windscreens were made in the village and the matter was sorted privately and instantly so the machine was kept on the road.

Bobbies did have accidents on them of course and this nearly happened to me returning from Bolton Abbey. As I rounded the bend at Farfield there was a hedgehog in my path. I have always been fond of hedgehogs' and I instinctively swerved. The machine went into a hop-skip-and jump, bounding along the road from side to side hopelessly out of control. I thought my end had come but then it righted itself of its own accord and I pulled in to recover.

Walking back to take the hedgehog to the roadside I found it was already dead from a previous collision so my attempt to save a dead animal had almost put me in a similar position. I resolved never to swerve for anything but human beings but of course we do for it is instinctive. Working a country beat means pheasants, grouse, partridges, rabbits, hares and sheepdogs are for ever crossing one's path and on the unfenced moorland roads sheep have the habit of waiting until you are near then stepping delicately into your path. One old farmer reckoned the Scottish black-faced-Swale dale cross breed did it deliberately!

The part of the beat up the Skipton-Harrogate road passed Deer stones and Storriths towards Pace Gate where a kiosk stood and points were made for it was the beat boundary with Blubberhouses I noticed an old tup belonging farmer Peter Harrison. It had magnificent curly horns ideal for a walking stick. The ram looked very unwell and being Diseases of Animals Inspector I called on

Peter and asked him if the ram died could I have the horns.

"Tup won't die," said Peter emphatically.

Next day I received a phone call from Mr. Harrison.

"Tup's died; if you want the horns be quick for I need to bury it."

I thanked him and said I would be up shortly needing to visit one of his neighbours over a dispute. A case of mixing business with pleasure I suppose.

As I drove back to the station through Farfield I came round the blind bend where the dead hedgehog had almost brought me to grief when I came across a horrific road accident which had just occurred. A saloon car had driven head on into a lorry full of stone. The lorry driver carried the two young children to the roadside and I struggled to free the parents who were both trapped. I had already radioed for assistance including the fire brigade and ambulance immediately on my arrival and they were soon on the scene.

It seemed the lady driver had pressed the accelerator pedal instead of the brake. At least I was there when most needed just because I had been for the rams horns. The occasions when this sort of thing occurred were too much of a coincidence and I was glad of that. That morning I could have gone anywhere and yet I was on the scene within seconds of the accident happening. Such cases are too numerous to mention but I will mention two.

One evening whilst passing the Wesleyan church a lady from one of the cottages saw me by the light of the street lamp and rushed out. She told me she had not seen her neighbour that day which was unusual and was worried. There was no reply to knocking and no sign within so I placed my cape over the back window and smashed it with my truncheon gaining entry.

The old lady was lying on a cold flag floor in her night clothes unconscious and cold as ice. As the ambulance drove away I was thinking that was the end of another village character and staunch Methodist of old farming stock. I paid for Mr. Dixon the joiner to repair the window for I had broken it and to submit a report was just adding to the overburdened bureaucratic system. Paper work was the bane of the service and was preventing 'proper' police work, i.e. 'the protection of life and property, the maintenance of order and the prosecution of offenders against the Peace'. Even a simple road accident would result in hours of typing up a prosecution file if an offence of driving without due care etc. was committed. Finding this lady would require only a brief entry in the occurrence book.

A week later patrolling in Main Street as the bus came in from Skipton I was gladdened but amazed to see Mrs Thackrey stepping off unaided. She gave a big smile and thanked me. Sometimes it's nice to be wrong about someone's anticipated demise but I didn't mention that to her!

Another elderly farm worker, Miss Garnett, complained about children troubling her in her council bungalow. I promised I would speak to them which I did remembering how we had been at their age during the build up to Mischief Night. In our time there was an imaginary witch on every street who kept a cat. When I grew up I learned they were widows of men killed in the Great War but we too must have been a nuisance. This poor lady had lived in isolation out on the farm and couldn't acclimatise to village life and the children had picked up on this slight difference in her.

A week after speaking to the children who promised to be 'good'! I was back on day duty walking near Miss Garnett's home when I thought to call and ask if the matter was resolved. There was no reply to my knock and a neighbour said she hadn't seen her the day before. There was a light on in the bedroom but the curtains were drawn. Looking through the kitchen window I could just see her figure sitting in a chair slumped over the table. She appeared to be dead.

The doctor's house and surgery were nearby so I hurriedly made my way over his garden wall knowing he would be setting off on his rounds about then. He came straight away and as before I broke the back window, climbed through and opened the kitchen door. The lady was just alive but very weak and quite unconscious. As she was carried away I asked the doctor what he thought of her chances and he shook his head. I didn't think there was a hope either.

Within a week she was home and shopping at Dixon's butchers so we were both wrong. I was learning that elderly Addingham ladies were made of tough stuff. Mind you they had lived through two world wars and still had the survival instinct. She lived for many a day but it was a near thing and had I not gone that way who knows!

On evening patrol on Mischief Night I rounded the corner at the Methodist church to see a medium sized homemade bomb smouldering in the middle of the road. The culprit was known to me and immediately ran into the school grounds where I cornered him on the steps. Ascertaining the ingredients I removed the device to the ditch and gave him one good dressing down. Fortunately he had got the mixture wrong or it could have been very serious and he most certainly would have been arrested and locked up but no damage was caused. Many boys like to experiment with explosives; I know we did just after the war but at that time all the ingredients could be bought at the chemist, in our case from Harold Wade at Aireworth Road. Miraculously we all survived!

Chapter 27

The Petrol Bomb

If someone suffering from a mental illness refused to take the medication and was deteriorating the old doctor would ask me to accompany him on his visit. With this particular patient it had happened several times over the years when Mr. B was eventually persuaded to go into hospital until he was well again. This time it was a little different for he met us outside his house in a very uptight, agitated state. He would not listen to us and when he produced a vicious looking knife we revived the Dunkirk spirit and retreated.

We returned the following day with another officer and the Mental Welfare Officer but the patient had locked himself in the house. His old mother was at my home being consoled by my wife who was familiar with the routine.

There was a downstairs window ajar so my colleague P.C. Alan Arnott, ex Royal Navy, climbed on my shoulders and got through, opening the front door and letting us all in.

The patient was in a small sitting room with the television going full blast and the electric fire fully on. It was impossible to talk to Mr B who was still most agitated, hopping from one foot to the other. I asked if I could turn the television off and as he wouldn't speak I switched it off and in doing so switched off the electric fire.

In a few moments I realised the importance of what I had done for Mr B produced a large glass bottle full of petrol from behind the settee where he was standing. It was meant to be smashed into the electric fire and had that happened it is not likely any of us would have survived in that small enclosed room. In frustration at the fire being out Mr B brought the glass bottle down over the head of the Mental Health Officer, showering him with petrol and shards of broken glass, stunning the poor man. We secured the patient and cleaned up the medic. We knew we had experienced a narrow escape.

Within a fortnight Mr B was back home leading his normal life and full of apologies for his bad behaviour. This was a man who was not ill until he was forty who had an important job, a happy family and was a sportsman. The illness robbed him of all that forcing him to live with his parents with all the attendant stress falling on that elderly couple. It was a sad case but one of many resulting from this troubled world.

Years later I was dealing with a sudden death at the hospital where the Mental Welfare Officer was now a senior official speaking to a group of nurses. On seeing me he turned to them and said,

"You see this man here – he saved my life; but for him I would not be talking to you now!"

I was not so sure about that but I am sure like the song 'Wild Mountain Thyme' we would all have gone together! Fate again for I didn't know the fire would have been put out when the television was switched off. No one can prepare for these happenings. Round every corner there was something different and danger was just another part of it to be taken in our stride.

Another mental patient falling to take his medication decided to set fire to the inside of his own ground-floor flat. The Fire Brigade had to travel from Ilkley so usually I was the first on the scene as I was in this case. The man was known to me but was clearly unresponsive to reason as I spoke to him through the broken windows. He was dressed only in his underpants and moving from room to room setting fire to anything that would burn. There were several gas bottles in the kitchen and as the Fire Brigade had not arrived I felt I had no choice but to go into the fire and bring the man out.

He was like a wild dog and tried to draw me more into the flames so I picked him up bodily, carried him outside and sat on him until a neighbour brought a blanket to wrap round him. By then the ambulance arrived and he was taken away.

We had very few house fires in the village and often I would muse on the money the villagers would save if they had their own Insurance Company and what they could do with that saving for the Common Good but the involvement with National Companies is now well ingrained and timid people are reluctant to change where risk is involved. What became of the 'Mutual Societies' one may ask?

The Strid at Bolton Abbey was on our beat, a place well known to tourists and those who wished to end their lives in spectacular style as some did every year. The river Wharfe narrows at a rocky point down in the woods. Even on a fine sunny day some find the place eerie and foreboding. At one point it is so narrow it is possible to leap across the chasm from one shelf of rock to another on the other side at a slightly lower angle. Often they are mossy and slippery which has been the undoing of many a daring young life. I have only known of three people getting out alive after falling in.

One of these was a lady teacher visiting the beauty spot with a group of other teachers. She wasn't even trying to jump the Strid, just walking alongside with the others when she slipped in and was carried away on the fast current. But for the quick thinking of a male member of the party who ran like the wind to get ahead of her she would have been carried under and drowned. As she swept by him he grabbed her by the hair and held on until his colleagues arrived and pulled her out.

The second case was attempted murder when a husband pushed his wife in and assuming she would be drowned went off to raise the alarm saying she had fallen in.

By a strange quirk of fate the wife was washed out of the maelstrom into calm water and crawled onto dry land, very shocked and frightened. When my colleague arrived she told him that her husband had tried to murder her by pushing her into the river. The lady was taken to the farm at the Ridding's, wrapped in blankets and sat by the warm fire. Meanwhile the husband had told his false tale to the Police and was even then down at the Strid showing where it had happened unaware that they knew his wife was fit and well in the nearby farm.

When the husband entered that kitchen and saw his wife drinking a large brandy he went the colour of death but did not faint. Although it was attempted murder this was a time when a spouse could not be compelled to give evidence against her husband so he escaped the law but whether he escaped the wrath of his wife we never knew and whether the marriage survived I know not but doubt how such as he could ever feel safe again in such a household but then, who knows!

The third occasion involved me and the sergeant when we received a message that a man was about to commit suicide at the Strid and we set off with me driving the mini-van. Whether Sergeant Chapman, a London cockney who had served throughout the war in the Royal Air Force, did not like travelling at speed in the flimsy van I wasn't sure.

"What's the hurry, Ken?" he asked.

"We want to save him, surely?" I said, reducing my speed very slightly!

"Oh, no," said the Sergeant, "Give him time if that's what he wants to do let him get on with it!"

Surely he's joking I thought but then he'd lived through the blitz and perhaps he didn't think much of those selfishly throwing their lives away when he'd seen so many lose their lives in enemy action!

Because of the frequency of Strid visits we had a key to the gate and were soon at the scene where the would-be suicide was sitting beneath a tree, fully clothed but soaked through, drinking from a half-full bottle of whisky. Beside him was a bag containing other spirits. He was from Leeds and suffering from depression but was otherwise unharmed. From what he said it appeared he had jumped in to end it all but the current had not dragged him down but carried him through to a sandy beach where he'd crawled out and resumed his drinking for another attempt.

"Told you we should give him time," said the Sergeant, "Now what are you going to do with him?"

"Get him some dry clothes at my place then take him to the Rector!" I said.

"The Rector won't want him; they don't like suicides," said the Sergeant.

"You'll see," I said, "This Rector has a kind Christian streak in spite of his other failings. He'll take care of him and see he gets home tomorrow."

We bundled the half-cut passenger into the back of the tiny van and carried out the plan. A few days later a parcel arrived at my station addressed to me. Freshly pressed and laundered clothing I'd given the man with a note of thanks for arranging accommodation at the Vicarage.

At that time there was no provision to deal otherwise with the likes of him. When I joined the Police suicide was a felony and attempted suicide a misdemeanour but that was repealed and rightly so.

The Strid usually gave up its victims from beneath the rocky shelves then the river carried them down to a pool near the Abbey. One victim from that pool received an open verdict for there were injuries to the head that may have been caused when he fell, jumped or, highly unlikely, was pushed in!

Just up from the Strid stands an oak tree that would have been alive when the Normans invaded our land over 800 years ago. It has been dying these last three hundred years a bit like it took the Roman Empire to fade after invasion and over population by other tribes. It sort of puts things in perspective but I wonder how long we've got?

Chapter 28

A Strange Wartime Tale

Jack and Donald Wood ran the blacksmith's forge and filling station at Bolton Abbey. Another brother was water bailiff. They were all fine, intelligent, useful fellows with many a tale to tell. Often have I thawed out in the forge when frozen stiff on the walk from Addingham to make a point outside their work place!

The three brothers all went off to the war but one brother stayed behind working at Catghyll Farm with Farmer Demaine. Early on in the war Mr Wood and Mr Tiffany were working in the farm yard. It was a bright clear day and they were watching two aeroplanes high in the blue engaged either in a dog-fight or a practice with machine guns. Suddenly Mr. Wood fell to the ground mortally wounded from a round from one of the planes. This was peaceful Bolton Abbey; a far cry from the conflict of war, yet it happened. Was the machine gun bullet from one of theirs or one of ours or was it an unfortunate training exercise that went wrong. Being wartime details were usually kept secret from the public so as not to damage morale. All Mr Wood's brothers, Donald, Jack and Harry returned safely home and lived on the estate for the rest of their lives.

Still early in the war a Spitfire was lost in the fog between Addingham and Ilkley and was seen by locals circling around for a considerable time until the pilot bailed out ,landing with his parachute on Ilkley Golf Course where the Home Guard took care of him. The Spitfire crashed into Cocking End Wood near Wallbanks farm and is believed to be there to this day, minus its wings which were removed by the authorities. It is believed the plane was from Evington near York. Incidentally, that wood was planted in 1917 by Harry Duckett of Addingham.

 The water bailiff, Harry Newbold, who reared trout for the estate up at Hazelwood came to see me in a bit of a panic. He'd learned that the Council were to carry out road repairs and widening on the Storriths-Hazlewood Road near his home and he was fearful for he and other boys during WW2 had buried a number of live anti-tank shells in the ditch at the side of the road where the improvements were to take place.

He showed me where they were buried and was emphatic about the location and the truth of the matter. I remembered what happened when some grouse beaters had thrown stones at an antitank shell which exploded with disastrous consequences on a nearby moor so the Bomb Disposal unit at Strensall Barracks were sent for.

They were searching for the elusive shells for four days during a very warm period. I called periodically to see their progress. There they were at Hazelwood; a sergeant major and three sappers of the Royal Engineers, stripped to the waist methodically digging, probing as if it were 1943 at El Alamein, about the time the shells were hidden. At least they acquired a good tan from their dales outing.

In the end they returned to barracks without finding a thing and the old water bailiff is still puzzled but there has been no explosion yet.

From time to time unexploded bombs were located on the moor, often seen after heather burning. Always we erred on safety and called out Bomb Disposal to deal with them. For several days I had a hand grenade in a bucket of water in the police house garden, perhaps a left-over from the Home Guard.

During WW2 the whole of this area after Dunkirk was a training ground for the Invasion on D Day. 15th Scottish Division were here with many famous regiments scattered around: the Cameronians in Keighley, the Highland Light Infantry at Bingley, The Argyll and Sutherland Highlanders and the Gordon Highlanders at Otley, the Royal Scots Fusiliers at Knaresborough and the Scots Guards at Ingleton.

They formed what was known as the Scottish Corridor, the breakthrough of the enemy lines in Normandy. We cannot imagine the casualties they suffered but the local training paid off and they achieved their objective and helped to bring the war to an end the following year. Some of these men married local girls; a few joined the West Riding Constabulary and useful men they were too.

The Durham Light Infantry was a tough regiment when on active service and one of its ex-members was just as tough farming at Bolton Abbey. Bronté Haworth was the proverbial fighting bantam cock and would not let any sleight pass without a challenge or a punch on the nose. Regardless of that, he was much admired as one of the hardest-working farmers on the estate and his wife and daughters were a credit to him for they shared his energy for work but fortunately lacked his pugnacious spirit.

Bronté had a milk round as well as his sheep and pigs and for some reason got into a disagreement with another milkman farmer called Mr Moon. It came to a head when Bronté pursued his rival for custom down the Harrogate Road in his Land Rover, stopped it and gave the driver a punch on the nose through the window. Mr Moon did not complain to me but as always in Bolton Abbey I heard about it and had to bring the quarrel to an end before Bronté really got himself in trouble. No sooner had I settled one dispute than another broke out over sheep with another neighbour Charlie, president of the 8th Army Association locally. Now Charlie was a big strong man but like the rest of them he was wary of Bronté and tried to avoid him.

When some sheep disappeared and others were found dead and mutilated Bronté immediately jumped to the conclusion that Charlie was responsible and reported it to me. Keeping an open mind I walked up to Charlie's remote farm and had a little chat. Not convinced that he was responsible and to keep Bronté happy I said I would make further enquiries and without telling anyone kept the dead sheep in view as I sat against the wall in shadow. After all I was Diseases of Animals Inspector and the sheep could have died from anything though I suspected the culprit was more likely to be canine.

It was quite pleasant in the peace and quiet with just the evening birdsong and distant sounds of curlews and peewits from the moor. A magpie came down for a look at the carcase and pecked out the accessible eye then flew away. Perhaps it had wind of me for I had not moved. Always it is movement that gives the game away to any quarry, animal or human.

The light was now fading fast and an owl flew silently by then I saw it, a large, lean, hungry looking Alsatian type dog. I felt justified in bringing the rifle and released the safety catch. To be more sure this was the culprit I allowed it to indulge itself in ripping out the throat of the sheep it had killed that morning then dispatched it with a single shot. The sound reverberated round the valley and all the cock pheasants in the area protested at the sound.

It turned out the dog had been living wild on the moor for several weeks. It had no collar and Bronté could not place it. The other missing sheep turned up on an adjoining farm no doubt having been chased by the same dog.

It was once quite common for domestic dogs to quit their home and go feral in the spring when lambing started. I suppose it was the wolf in them that came to the fore. Certainly they could cause a lot of damage and some farmers would shoot a dog on sight before it had even looked at a sheep.

My shooting partner, a constable in charge of the Hebridean island of Barra had only been there a few days when a crofter asked him to help with two collies worrying his sheep. Jack accompanied the man who pointed out the dogs far away on a distant hill. Jack got into the kneeling position with his rifle and told the crofter to whistle. On hearing the whistle the two dogs stopped and turned. Two shots rang out and that problem was solved. Jack's reputation as a crack shot spread round the island like wildfire and thereafter he was in great demand.

In all Jack shot 27 dogs worrying livestock in the four years he was there and gained a degree at the Open University. They were very law-abiding people on Barra! No ship laden with whisky was wrecked on the rocks as in WW2 as described in Compton McKenzie's book Whisky Galore. I think had I been there at that time I would have let them have the lot. They certainly earned their quota after diving into the deep hold to recover the stuff. Officialdom can be very stupid at times! Keen countrymen with good eyesight notice things more than the average person and often have a sixth sense about things. My friend had that.

Travelling down the A9 from Inverness to Aviemore where it is open heather and forest to the left all the way to the Cairngorms Jack glimpsed something on the ground a few hundred yards out from the road. He travelled several more miles before he convinced himself he ought to go back. It was as well he did for when he walked across the rough moor he could see it was a young woman who was in a collapsed state. He alerted his colleagues and ambulance and she was removed to hospital.

She had been missing several days from a psychiatric ward and was suffering from exposure. Jack had found her just in time for she could not have survived another night.

Chapter 29

Fishy Tales

Below Draughton Lane there is a free-flowing trout stream and whenever I passed that way I could not resist stealing up to the parapet of the bridge to slowly look over to see if any trout were about. One bright sunny day I did just that and was rewarded by seeing a fine, brown trout, hovering in the current facing up stream. My mind went back to the spring of 1946 with my father newly demobbed from the army and with my mother as well enjoying my first holiday in a Gypsy caravan at Arncliffe. Tickling trout had always been a pastime of my family, both in Scotland and Yorkshire and in the tributaries of the Skerfare there were plenty.

As I watched this solitary specimen on my own beat the primitive instincts were at play so I climbed the wall and crept to the water's edge to see the big fish go under the bank. That was the cue. Off came the helmet and tunic and with sleeves rolled up to the armpits I lay on the grass bank and felt beneath. My fingers soon touched the familiar slippery scales of Salmo trutta which I found just as exciting as my first contact in a stream near Loch Lomond but could I capture the fish, I wondered. All other thoughts had left my mind; the legality of fishing without a licence, the law and all the unnatural selfish worldly things. For a few moments I was like my ancestors.

Slowly I slid my fingers up to the gills and the head and then lifted the one and a half pounder from his pool. Just for seconds I admired his red and black spots, his silver scales and beautiful eye then slid him back into his kingdom. That was enough; I could not have killed that fish; I didn't need to anymore; he had a right to be there. As I donned my tunic and helmet I wished him well that the Heron would not get him but again, that was nature too, just like me!

When a coach-load of miners from Barnsley way arrived down at the pavilion at Bolton Abbey they caused a flurry of excitement among the ticket staff for everyone had a creel and a fishing rod. They quickly dispersed to both banks of the river and assembled their tackle. They wasted no time making their first casts so perhaps they knew of the panic they would be causing to the, as yet, absent water bailiffs.

Receiving a call from the estate office I set off unaware they were coal miners at this stage. Now I've always had a lot of time for miners for without their dangerous toil underground we could not have survived two world wars. Traffic was busy so it was some time before I got there which was just as well for it was quite a party and tensions were high. All the miners were gathered by the bridge over the Wharfe along with the water bailiffs and the Duke's agent. Nearby, on the grass lay all their fishing rods and creels. The miners had paid for their ticket to come in to the estate field and assumed that gave them the right to fish. The agent shook his head.

"Well," said one miner indignantly, "I've been fishing this river for the past year and nobody's said owt to me about it being private. I caught some good trout too."

There was a murmur from the rest and even the agent had to smile.

I could see the men had been angling in the daytime without authority but they did have river board licences and whilst their colleague's tale of fishing freely for a year was a bit cheeky I could see some real problems arising if the estate took them to court. For one thing, the tackle, when seized had not been labelled to the angler using it. None of it had; it just lay in a heap and without their cooperation which I could not imagine being given, any case would fall flat.

I spoke to the agent in private and suggested he obtain a promise from the miners that they would not fish here again. In return their gear would be returned, minus trout, and no further action would be taken. The anger dissipated, the miners promised and off they set for Kilnsey Trout Farm where they had heard some trout weighed up to twelve pounds!

The finest fisher of all is the heron, that tall, gray, pre-history-like bird with strong beak and beady eye that stands on one leg like a statue on the riverside waiting for its prey. Of course, fishing becoming such a lucrative thing for those landowners blessed with a river through their land are not always happy to see such big birds doing what they have always done, namely eating fish. There are fewer herons about these days but I once knew a heronry of seventeen pairs on an estate at Gargrave and a good sized one down the Wharfe near Askwith. There is a place for all surely or that is what I thought when coming across magnificent specimens shot and hidden in a ditch by someone with a vested interest in killing them. Always such offences come to light sooner or later!

One heron found shot through one wing at Barden was taken in by a lady teacher at Silsden. She went to endless trouble for that bird providing it with its correct diet of fish in her living room which smelled like a heronry. All birds when hungry and injured become tame and this bird got to know her and responded at feed times with some very strange noises. It was released into the wild and I do believe she had been successful with her nursing. Like most of our generation we were brought up to be kind to dumb animals!

Near to the Strid was Barden Beck Bridge, our beat boundary with Grassington Section. Receiving a radio call of a road accident there I set off from Beamsley.

As usual I was not far from the scene. A young farmer driving his Land Rover had collided with a car driven by an old man on the bridge. The farmer was unhurt but the old man was in a state of shock and bleeding quite badly.

From day one on the beat I carried two triangular bandages in my inside pocket for such emergencies and each day in my left trouser pocket a freshly laundered cotton handkerchief, not to be confused with the one in my right pocket for my own use. So many times they had been useful when far out from immediate assistance and this was one such case. I had radioed for an ambulance from the 'Noddy Bike' now a useful tool in rural policing and a vast improvement on the pedal cycle.

The bleeding was stemmed as far as I could manage but the poor man looked very ill and I feared he would not last until the arrival of the ambulance. We waited an hour at the side of the road before it came. It was not an official ambulance but a part-time St. John's ambulance from Grassington. Never-the-less the farmer and I were very relieved to see him go to hospital.

The St. John's Ambulance Brigade did much good training first aiders and as a youth I too had benefitted from their medical skills when inevitable injuries occurred. Most West Riding police officers were trained by them in first aid and we were grateful for that.

The young farmer later died in a shocking road accident on the A1 and was a great loss to the community.

As regards road accidents there was scarcely a yard of those roads that I had not dealt with one, sometimes fatal but usually with some injury or other; then there were the miraculous escapes with a vehicle smashed to bits and no one hurt. The road improvements to the A59 and the A65 certainly have made a difference but accidents still occur!

Chapter 30

A Wintry Tale

Davey was the epitome of the 'canny shepherd laddie of the hills' from the song of that name, living high up on the ridge of Addingham Moorside where in the winter the snow and frost lingered because the sun never reached that part of the hill in winter. His grazing land extended over the moor to join with the parish of Silsden and Ilkley and it was there I would often come across him herding his sheep or perhaps hear him calling his dog in the mist when bringing them off the moor when snow threatened.

The moor for me was a place of solitude; somewhere to go to find temporary peace, to watch the ring ouzel and curlews in spring; to find a grouse nest or just to breathe the clean air away from the toxic fumes of motor cars with all their problems. The moors had been my playground since boyhood, rebuilding grouse butts and burning heather with the keepers, catching rabbits for the pot. The moor was a good place but in winter it could be a dangerous killer.

Years before, when about twelve years old I was out on the moor alone when a blizzard blew up. It was exciting and already I had shot a hare and hoped to get another so I sat under a wall to wait for a hare to appear down the moorland track. I was comfortable and felt strangely warm considering the low temperatures and the swirling snowflakes in the strong wind. The light was fading and so was I. Sleep was creeping over me but some instinct told me to get up and move myself. I knew about Captain Scott's polar expedition and their loss in these conditions, particularly Titus Oates who went off into the blizzard to die to make it easier for his comrades. I was hardly ready for that at twelve but that little foretaste of how it would be put the wind up me and I went home having learned a lesson for life!

On such a cold snowy afternoon Davey was bringing his sheep down off the high moor after a fall of snow the previous day with more threatened when he saw the figure of a man sitting against the wall below the footpath to the Noon Stone and Swastika Rock. The man was elderly and appeared to have died there. He telephoned my home station.

On receipt of his message a colleague and I went up. Rigor mortis had set in and there was no means of identification. We carried the poor chap down on our backs to the waiting hearse for it was nearly dark and there was no easy way to get him off the rocky slope. At the mortuary we could find nothing to identify the man but we laid him out and made him tidy knowing there must be a relative somewhere worried about him.

The day following I began enquiries and the first shop I went into was the Co-op in Bolton Roar asking if the staff knew if anyone was missing. No one did but as I left a lady asked to speak to me privately and explained her brother had been missing two days. The story she told was a sad one. She and her brother had lived with their parents in the same terraced house and continued living there after their parents died. All through those years they had paid their rent regularly then the landlord sold the property to someone the locals called a 'hippy'.

Several 'hippy' types came to live in the village at that time, seeking to be self-sufficient, smoking cannabis and worse! A number of old Addingham families moved away because of the disruption they caused and the sort of people they were bringing into the community. The story is as old as the hills the world over but apart from drug taking and lesser offences which seemed to be gaining acceptance they hovered on the perimeter of the law. Their lifestyle was not real and they were either of independent means or on social security, most likely the latter.

The new owner of their home informed them they would have to find other accommodation. Naturally this greatly upset the couple, the older brother particularly, which caused him to go to the moor on a freezing day to sit and wait for death. He would not have had to wait long up there but it was outrageous that he should have been driven to that. The person responsible for causing the upset was from a good home, was educated but obsessed with 'attacking the under belly of the state' and determined to get their home for his friends.

The cause of death was exposure and the Coroner was not pleased how the old man had been treated.

The same individual put some 'underground literature' through my letterbox with sheets of paper impregnated with LSD which I am told could be absorbed through the skin when handling it! I also found a large crop of Cannabis plants in an area few people went. I retained a specimen beneath my blotter for years to show young policemen what to look out for as it was getting widespread.

Occasionally someone was sent to prison for possessing drugs or dealing with them, even the odd one coming from Holland with a consignment and the penalties could be severe but not always fair.

A young man from a Silsden council estate was sentenced to nine months imprisonment for possessing cannabis whilst in the same week in a London court a music celebrity was ordered to pay a small fine for much the same thing. The Law is so easily brought into disrepute!

Eventually the 'hippy' sold up and moved away. I heard he was very ill and not expected to live so I went to see him. Clearly he was dying but he received his old adversary as friendly as ever and apologised for how he had behaved towards me and others. I was glad of that. He died within the week!

Most of the 'hippy' tribe drifted away as the novelty wore off and the odd ones who stayed merged into the part of the community that suited their needs!

The Scottish soldiers who were billeted here during the war left no appreciable damage to the fabric of the village and likely improved it with the inevitable influx of fresh blood into the gene pool for it is a wise father who knows his own child!

By comparison the period of the hippies did little or nothing for the community and passed away into oblivion. They looked upon the police force as fascists yet without them they would have been thrown to the wolves and there were people in the village who would have quite liked that.

Attending with some 500 other officers at a National Front rally I immediately noticed a man from the village. He looked very smart in his black leather jerkin but was greatly embarrassed at me seeing him. The rally was a rough affair with our contingent trying to hold back the International Socialist and various other groups determined to attack the Front supporters and us, the peacekeepers right in the middle of the opposing sides. The worst of it was the missiles being thrown at the horses behind us; none of this was their fault.

Most of the time our arms were linked which made us very vulnerable and my friend Malcolm next to me, a former Black Watch soldier, was incensed at the insults and desperate to get up and at them as his forebears had done at Killiekrankie. It took two police pipers to restrain him and point out the cameras and the taunts were done to cause us to break ranks and attack the mob. We never did and the hullabaloo was over as quickly as it began. Sometime after, the National front steward explained it was just a phase he was going through and that it had passed!

I sometimes think, if people were truthful, they diverge in the course of a day from rampant fascist to benevolent tory to damp-eyed liberal and sharing socialist back on to blood red communists plus all the other isms between. Politics is a minefield. We all have our views and from my experience we should understand politics but as police officers never get involved. Each officer will see enough daily problems but if you have doubts read George Bernard Shaw's Guide to the Isms or go to Belsen and see the mass graves!

H H

Chapter 31

A New Home

The day before we moved into the police house with office in Church Street alongside the Main Road, we fitted a new carpet in the lounge. The morning after we discovered someone had thrown a large stone through the window causing sharp pieces of glass to fly everywhere. It took some clearing up without a vacuum cleaner but we had to be sure for our baby daughter was just eleven months old. I could not imagine who had done it but over a period of time a pattern emerged.

A small boy living nearby had been caught by Jimmy Hadley smashing every pane in his greenhouse. Mr Hadley knew the circumstances of the boy and didn't want a prosecution but I did speak to the boy and he could give no explanation for committing the damage nor to my window, which he admitted to. I tried to involve the boy with others in the neighbourhood but he did not easily mix. He got into various scrapes.

One day I was called to the river where the lad had been watching a fisherman fishing in deep water when without any warning the boy collapsed and went face down to the bottom. The angler managed to get him out of the river but he was still unconscious when I arrived. I carried him up the steep bank to the ambulance and he was taken to hospital. He was diagnosed with epilepsy and warned he must not go near the river.

He started taking motor cars, was brought before the court by police in another area and sent to a Young Offenders Institution from which he escaped along with three others. I was due in court that day but heard from a neighbour that the four had barricaded themselves in the bedroom of his home. Knowing I was required in court I borrowed a ladder, placed it below the bedroom window and tried to reason with him. They were full of bravado and it was clear they were not going to give themselves up.

The expression on their faces when I smashed their window with my staff and went into the room was an interesting one. They clearly had not expected me to do that but I did need to get to court for more important matters. Then the boy drew a knife which I knocked out of his hand. With the arrival of Sergeant Chapman they were soon taken into custody and returned to the Institution and I left for court in Skipton before anything else cropped up.

For several years pieces of my garden fence would be broken off but for me there was nothing serious from this young man though there was for him.

A man came banging on my door to say there was a body in the river. My fence was no longer damaged after that. It was a great shame but people other than me had tried to help him and even with the advice about the river he had taken no notice.

There were a few similar cases for some young men think they are immortal. If only they knew the grief it would causes their parents and family.

One who had come to my notice on a motor bike, riding at excessive speed presented an opportunity when he was smoking outside the youth club. I spoke quietly to him so the other members wouldn't hear and told him he would end up killing someone unless he got his act together. He said little but at least he left his bike behind that night for I saw him waiting for the bus as I went for my supper.

I invited him to join me and bought fish and chips for the pair of us. At home my wife made some tea and I tried to discover what the youth wanted to do. He spoke of going to sea so when he left I gave him some books on the navy and he left on good terms. He was killed in a motor cycle crash not long after.

Another bright young lad driving like there was no tomorrow came to notice and was prosecuted for dangerous driving. When producing his documents I had a good talk with him for I knew his parents. I spoke to his father and expressed my fears that he would end up killing himself. He did!

On Easter Tuesday I dealt with a six vehicle accident on the New Road by Cocking End when a sports car driven by a 21 year old university student collided with various others. He was killed immediately and an elderly lady coming in the opposite direction was also killed; a number of others were injured. The sports car finished up squarely on top of another car in Cocking End junction. Had it been placed there by a crane it could not have been more exact. A witness said there was a blue flash as it hit the first car.

Sergeant Chapman laid out the body in the mortuary at Ilkley, bathing away the grit and dirt to make him presentable for his poor father who would have to identify him.

I could speak of many more incidents like these where young men are involved. As every parent knows the growing up phase is a dangerous time. I sometimes think young people of a certain age should be taken to the mortuary and made to see where reckless actions lead. I think only shock tactics with some is the only way. It may seem drastic but it may just save a lot of grief!

For years the husband of the lady who was killed in that accident would call to see me and my wife would make him at home. I suppose he saw me as the last person to have any link with his wife before she passed away at the scene. Life can be very cruel at times and people can be very cruel which has always amazed me. A trip to the mortuary might steady some!

With the issue of the first two-way radios, albeit in two separate halves, one for each pocket, we no longer had to make points at public telephone kiosks but the beat covered a very wide area and there were many blank spots where no signal could be transmitted. I discovered one such when working at Bolton Abbey one weekend. A hiker reported an elderly walker had broken his leg up above the Valley of Desolation and gave me good directions. Knowing the area well I set off to find him but was unable to get a message back to Ilkley to arrange the Fell Rescue team. The radio would not work.

On finding the man I made him comfortable and confirmed he had slipped whilst descending the rough path and indeed his leg was broken but he was not stressed and was content to await the rescue team. First I had to tell them where we were.

In the process of sending out unanswered messages I started picking up strong Geordie accents and began trying to engage them saying I was dealing with an emergency. During a lull in their air traffic I made contact and they kindly informed Ilkley and the Fell Rescue of our location. The wonders of modern science! I could not reach the Ilkley aerial which I could see from the high hill on which we sat, yet I could pick up Newcastle Police Headquarters in Northumberland. Thanks to their intervention the man was soon carried away to hospital.

Late one evening I was sitting in our new home in Church Street when we heard someone call my name from the street outside, then shout for help. It was one of our Parish Councillors.

He had attended a meeting at the 'Old School' in Main Street and set off home when he noticed some men watching him by the Crown Hotel. He continued walking down past the Fleece aware they were in a van, slowly following him. He headed for my home and fortunately I was there which was when we heard him shouting.

As I ran outside one of the men stole his briefcase and ran to the van's open door where I tried to trap him to prevent his escape but they drove off towards Ilkley. Details were passed to Ilkley and the men apprehended, subsequently appearing in court.

The councillor was naturally shaken by the experience for there appeared no logical reason to pick on him but he soon got over it. At least he knew where to seek sanctuary in what for him was a frightening experience.

Chapter 32

Examinations

Examination passes were a prerequisite to promotion and whilst I was very happy working as a village bobby some senior officers encouraged me to take them. I studied hard and gained a very high pass mark in the Home Office law exams and top in the force but for half a mark. That officer had been an ex-cadet and his experience was working with Road Fund Licences. He was also only 24 years old. I believe he became an Assistant Chief Constable; I was thirty years old with eight years practical service plus my military service.

Some in the Home Office felt the police were not receiving their quota of graduates and began recruiting from those gaining high marks plus other suitability. As a result of this I went on the extended interviews in London and having got through that on to Churchill College, Cambridge.

One of the things we discussed was the Race Relations Bill going through its third reading. I said it was unnecessary, that the Public Order Act of 1936, if amended would be adequate. I also warned if the Race Relations bill became law it would not be long before we were discriminating against our own people and that would not be right.

My feelings were very strong on account of my father-in-law having just died at 57. An honourable man from the highlands who was the Regimental Sergeant Major of the Royal Scots; having been involved in fierce fighting in Burma for which he received the Distinguished Conduct Medal from the King on his return; a man who fought in the rear-guard at Dunkirk and escaped despite the odds.

There was a hippyish mood in the country with people forgetting what WW2 had cost us. Men had died fighting for the freedom of speech and I could see very soon it wouldn't just be the English dictionary having to change. What would Will Shakespeare think! Also that week the Russians had invaded Czechoslovakia so there were some heated debates.

Some of the other candidates had degrees already and in any case I knew before I went a degree course was out of the question as my wife had just given birth. I had seen good men promoted in the army and the police and none seemed to improve as men though I don't doubt they were good at their job. In the army, after privileged public school, many young subalterns had been to university but I knew of very few in the police in the North. It was this concern that brought us together or was it? Some of the finest agents had attended Cambridge and some of them worked for the Crown but the more famous ones did not. The board carrying out the interviews were clever men, some academics, some military with exemplary war records and other senior police officers plus the odd psychologist. We did not know it but within a short time the unsettled Irish problem would resurrect itself and the army and forces of law and order really would be put to the test. For the moment this was far from our minds.

The official that greeted my group in calling us together announced, "All the Communists over here!" It seemed an odd thing to say but again, I could not speak for the rest but I had twice tried to read Karl Marx 'Das Capital', was familiar with Tom Pain's 'The Rights of Man' and the 'Age of Reason' and the biography of Ramsay McDonald, Labour party leader and three times Prime Minister. In his case fame really was the spur, a bit like the Liberal leader Lloyd George and perhaps the most outstanding of his time, Sir Winston Churchill whom I had also studied. For good measure I had read Mein Kamp too and Fitzroy McLean, Montgomery and at great length the Jacobite Rising of 1745 plus countless other interesting books that grabbed my attention.

From the outset of the Cambridge interviews and the theme behind it to select suitable candidates to attend university, I had a dilemma. On the morning I was informed I had passed the exams our daughter was born. Now, I remember how it was when I was born and my father was away for six years fighting a war and the difficulties my mother went through without him. As advantageous as it might seem, I could not justify being away months or years in time of peace and create all the problems for my family that I had seen occur with other officers who had taken time out to go to university and then found it was too big a strain! I knew what I was good at and I was satisfied with that.

Although there were few graduates in the North there were plenty of intelligent men who in different circumstances would have automatically gone to university. The Cambridge candidates were of that ilk, were polite, well-mannered and some really did have the gift of the gab, more like politicians or lawyers than Bobbies. I felt privileged to be there and had I been six years younger would have jumped at a chance to study for three years or so but my family were settled and my wife would need me around. Ambition is a laudable thing but so is family. In any case it was experienced Bobbies on the beat that were needed; that was where the work was done in serving the people and that was something I knew a great deal of. Someone had to replace all the WW2 veterans who were retiring in large numbers.

The interview board asked many questions, some of them very awkward but perhaps the most awkward was 'Does the end justify the means'? I felt I answered that badly remembering I was trained to fight terrorism in the 50s. Had I been more honest I should have said, "If a man is in custody with knowledge of his comrades who are going to plant an explosive device which will kill and maim many innocent people and he knows where and when this will take place, what does one do?" If the intended victims are strangers it is one thing but if they are your family it is another. It is hard to face up to what should be done. It is possible to gain information without having to resort to torture and the British, unlike some continental neighbours, have always found torture abominable, but I confess I do not know the answer in this case. Obviously, there are cases where the end justifies the means. For instance, in warfare, to lose twenty men to save a hundred would be justified!

Five times I was offered promotion in the Police and once in the army. I declined all offers which puzzled some. One assistant Chief Constable asked me if I was of independent means producing some merriment. I explained I had reached the top of the tree on the bottom rung of the ladder and cheekily backed this up by saying I received correspondence addressed to the Chief Constable of Addingham.

Mr. Mogg, my Chief Superintendent on the last board I attended had the patience to listen to me. He was a good man, had served as a pilot in the Royal Air Force during the war then in the Control Commission in Germany. I told him straight that standards were falling yet the Chief Constable was saying we were short of men. I said I did not wish to be in a supervisory position because of falling standards for it was not what I was used to, that if I were in the Chief Constable's position he would be short of men for I would remove the dead wood and train up people who could be relied on.

He nodded and said we could only use the materials we already had to which I said, if the materials are faulty the whole structure would fall down around our ears. From where I stand today, that has happened. It seems the police force I knew has gone and what stands in its place is a force more concerned with its own professionalism than the welfare of the public. I would like to be wrong in this assumption for I still care for those men and women who try to do that job.

So I was left to work my beat and with reorganisation two officers were taken away to work elsewhere. Even my transport was taken and for five years I did what three officers had done! I was offered the post of instructor at Bishop Garth, the Force Training centre with immediate promotion; was told I should reach the rank of Chief Inspector at least. It didn't tempt me and I think my wife was relieved.

Chapter 33

Back to Basics

The Protection of Birds Act 1954 introduced by Lady Tweedsmuir, wife of the great writer John Buchan (of 39 Steps fame), was done with good intent for it coincided with massive changes in Britain's agriculture which were not conducive to bird life. Since the Act came in bird life for many species diminished alarmingly. To give some examples, before the Act I could find perhaps a dozen pewit nests in one field; in the course of a summer know of at least three young cuckoos in meadow pipit nest, wheatears and redstarts were common as were redpolls, linnets and yellow hammers to mention a few. Now they are virtually unknown in these dales.

There was no teaching of bird protection at the police colleges I attended yet it was the duty of the police to protect such and the birds, along with insects (such as bees) are perhaps the first creatures to indicate that all is not well with the World! The first prerogative of the police is the protection of life so perhaps when all Bobbies have been to university and understand the importance of all life there will be a change in attitude. I forget though, we must first get the Bobbies back!

The much credited film 'Kes' was an outstanding success for the producers and the stars in it. It was a film about a young working-class boy and his tame kestrel. Unfortunately, despite the bird protection law, it was a disaster for the kestrel population in Wharfedale and the surrounding area. Every boy wanted a kestrel and all the nests had the young stolen. It took Nature several years for the population to be restored. There was just one prosecution locally. Always, in the countryside there are people wise to making a quick shilling from wildlife and he wasted no time selling the young chicks.

On a visit to Skipton court I saw a kestrel flying about in the living room of a terraced house, flapping at the window trying to get out. The young lad said it had fallen out of its nest! How many times had I heard that tale relating to young birds, particularly hawks and owls! In my day we were content to tame jackdaws, jays and magpies, a plentiful species which made good pets which might have been shot by the gamekeepers.

The village of Addingham is famous for its large mallard duck population originally introduced to the village by David Myles and Gerald Fawcett from hand-reared stock. They multiplied as ducks are wont to do. Most people love them but not everyone and residents of Bark Lane were incensed when they saw a group of boys being cruel to them. Why some people do that is beyond me but

it occurs in individual sadistic beings from time to time and then the law
steps in.

A friend of mine from the Scottish Borders working the Riddlesden Beat over
the hill from Addingham was making a point at Cox's Corner opposite Victoria
Park when he saw two furtive looking lads pushing a bicycle and carrying a sack.
Like two junior Bill Sykes from Oliver Twist he asked them to empty the sack.
Out fell two dead swans, dirty and bloody minus their heads.

Duncan was a gentle soul but his instinct was to give both of them a good smack
but since the Wick ruling in Caithness, it was held that Bobbies did not have the
right to mete out corporal punishment and so he kept his hands to himself.

Mute swans are technically the property of the Crown; they are perhaps the
most graceful birds we have and bring endless pleasure to many. A society that
still produces destroyers of beauty really does have a problem but it has always
been so. Boys make dreadful mistakes during the course of growing up which
is how some learn but they can bring endless shame on themselves and their
families which means a harsh deterrent is necessary for everyone's sake! I am
not saying it has to be as fearsome as the military used to be but it does need
to be fearsome! However, you can't have detection without Bobbies and there
is nothing more useless for a Nation than to have innumerable laws it cannot
enforce which is our present state at the moment!

Early in my service I escorted two teenagers to a Young Offenders Prison in
Durham. They had been convicted of stealing cars. As we arrived we noticed
squads of lads being drilled unmercifully in the rain wearing football shorts
and vests. They weren't just being shouted at; they were being screamed at by
prison officers who were more like the army drill instructors who trained my
generation. It was un-nerving just as it had been when I was a teenage soldier
and I couldn't get out of that place of detention fast enough.

We handed the boys over and even in our close presence the staff shouted and
screamed at them to stand against the wall. The poor beggars were shaking with
fear. The signing over, we fled that place and I resolved never to escort anyone
there again if I could help it. This short, sharp shock treatment may have been
effective as a deterrent with the young and certainly the harsh training we
endured in the military did not appear to do any of us any harm but this is really
an area I am not qualified to speak on.

If a fox stole my hens I shot it; if a crow or a magpie stole my eggs I shot it;
if after all the training the state had given me, someone threatened the life of
anyone, I knew what to do. When you come down to the nitty-gritty it is basic
common-sense. Alas, there appears to be little about. Although I studied law up
to a high standard, gaining the highest mark in criminal law at that time, I was

told up to L.L.B. standard but I am glad I did not become a lawyer. From the old English song on the highwayman Dick Turpin on the legal profession, 'And first he robbed him of his score because he knew he'd lie for more'! Perhaps that is a little harsh and too general for I have known many in the legal profession and like the Germans they weren't all bad!

Two young chaps in the village were proud keepers of poultry, keeping them in a large wired-in run by the allotments then one morning when coming to feed them they were horrified to find them all mutilated and dead. Some did have their heads taken off such as a fox would do but I was not entirely convinced for we had people who were always envious and sometimes they would go to shocking lengths to spite others. If the owners suspected anyone they were not for telling me so by the process of elimination I would remove one suspect and see if I still had the skills to kill my quarry.

It was well known among poultry keepers that birds had to be fastened in at night or the fox would have them which was why so many had given up keeping poultry. The decline of gamekeepers meant fewer would reduce the fox population.

There was a covering of snow from the night before as I set off late that afternoon for the Moorside. I knew the earths the foxes were using but the tracks in the snow would confirm their presence. One such earth was clearly being used and I settled down to wait as darkness fell. Just as the light was nearly gone the fox left the earth and I shot her clean. My hands were almost too frozen to replace the safety catch.

As I passed his cottage at the Slade Peter Thompson invited me in for a drink of tea. I was glad of that for I had waited in the bitter east wind for a long time. So the Vixen would no longer take peoples hens, if it was the vixen!

Some crimes are never satisfactorily solved because of the lack of evidence even though our gut instinct points to the culprit but often the victims do know who is responsible yet will not disclose their name for reasons best known to them. It has always been thus! For me personally it didn't matter over much for I knew they would receive their reward in due course of time and that never failed!

Chapter 34

Out for a duck and other crimes

My wife knew my location when a neighbour reported to her that he had disturbed a gang of burglars at his home so I was quickly informed. A friend drove me to the office in his mini and I was able to pass on the registration number of the van being used. Two offenders had escaped in the van and one other wearing a yellow jacket had run towards the saw mill. Goods from the bungalow next to Hadley's Garage were stacked in the drive when the owner returned home.

Still in the mini my pal and I drove slowly passed the Fleece bus stop. At the end of the queue was a man without a jacket. It was freezing with a thick white frost which had been there for days. Clearly the conspicuous yellow jacket had been discarded. As I got within a yard of the suspect he bolted, running towards Hadley's Garage. As he rounded the bend he saw the police car pulling up so he threw himself over the thick thorn hedge into Billie Brear's field. I knew then we would corner him against the saw mill dam.

Climbing Mrs Bigland's wall I walked quietly across the lawn and crouched to listen. Sure enough the burglar was heading towards the dam. It was a still night and every move he made reverberated around the huge garden. Then the unexpected happened. There was a mighty splash and crash of breaking ice coupled with the loud quaking of dozens of ducks as they fled from their roost on the dam side. The game was almost up. His final desperate attempt to evade capture was to crawl into the stream culvert beneath Bolton Road. It was there we found him, soaked through, shivering with cold, a pathetic specimen of a thief. He was a good runner though and bearing that in mind I handcuffed him for the walk down Main Street to the transport.

All the burglars were caught, all the property recovered and no one was hurt except our runner! At court the next day he stood in the dock with a very black eye and swollen and cut face. I knew it was nothing to do with us but it looked bad.

"What happened to your face?" asked the Chairman of the Bench.

He grinned sheepishly as he stood between his two partners in crime.

"It was not the police, Sir, it was the ducks. When I fell in the dam I disturbed them and some flew up into my face." A rare ripple of laughter ran around the room.

The Chairman spoke again.

"Well, that's a relief but if the police have the ducks working for them as well in Addingham it clearly is not the place to go burgling!"

The radio message said the alarm had gone off at Hallcroft Hall some three hundred yards from where I stood. I ran the distance and arrived at the high wall around the late Dr Oddy's former mansion. Another message informed me that my colleague P.C. Bill Pitt had disturbed two men and was in pursuit towards the river. From my position I saw Bill gaining on one man who jumped in the river with PC Pitt close behind. The ex-Coldstream Guardsman dived in after him.

I joined Bill in the chase across farmer Mower's field when Bill brought him down with a rugby tackle. There followed a violent struggle to place the handcuffs on the man, now like a wild animal, spitting and snarling like a rat in a trap. His accomplice had escaped. He was wanted by the Metropolitan Police for attempted murder of a police officer by stabbing him in the stomach. They were both professional criminals arriving in our village by courtesy of the new motorway from London.

Bill received a commendation for his actions and rightly so. During the war the Coldstream's' had a reputation for taking no prisoners. Perhaps this fellow had a narrow escape! The stolen silver was all recovered wrapped in drapes ripped from the windows and left on the ground and at least one offender was brought to justice!

Low Mill was one of the oldest surviving of its kind in the country. The Luddites had paid a visit during the period of industrial unrest resulting in a squadron of dragoons being despatched too late to prevent damage to the boilers. A few shots were fired and I believe one protester was killed before the soldiers chased them back to Lancashire.

The modern part of the mill was still operational but lead was being stolen from its roof. Suspecting local thieves I went down late at night to try and catch them. Working alone at night had never troubled me from my boyhood days of long-netting and gate netting hares, sometimes on very dark nights. It was exhilarating and it kept one very fit and alert, able to distinguish the night sounds, training one to be on guard for the gamekeeper or farmer. All this would prove invaluable when military service came or as now, hunting for thieves. There was little difference except we killed hares and rabbits and ate them!

It was going on for midnight when I saw two figures padding down the side of the mill and disappearing round the back where a fire escape gave them access to the roof. I decided to wait until they came back confident they were locals and that they would come quietly when I challenged them and identified them.

Wearing my cape and tall helmet with the shiny badge I waited patiently thinking my patience would soon be rewarded. Just over the mill wall was the river Wharfe in full spate, making a great roaring sound as it sped by to join forces with the Ouse, the Humber and the Great North Sea!

I did not hear the men approaching because of the rushing water but suddenly they were on the wall, their silhouettes against the night sky. They were very close and saw the glint of my helmet badge. Switching on my night lamp I realised I had miscalculated for these were not locals. One was a big black fellow, the other a little white chap. I did not recognise either. Only for seconds was I forced into confronting them on top of the broken wall. In the circumstances I was glad they ran away.

The following day we traced the white chap to Bradford. He eventually went to prison for more serious offences. The black accomplice never was traced but I imagine he got a bit of a surprise finding a Bobbie in such a place in the middle of the night; I know I got a bit of a surprise too.

The Rhodesian crisis of the 1960's caused a big problem locally and it wasn't because many of us were on the Army reserve list and were half-expecting the British Government to intervene. Most of our copper came from that country and because of the shortage the price went sky high. Scrap metal dealers were working overtime processing illegally obtained copper from overhead cables where it was used as an earth.

A local gang operating from Skipton equipped with pickup vehicles and ladders seemed invincible in spite of some close encounters with the police. One such was at Silsden near the canal in spring at the time a farmer had gone out to check the lambing. He had a narrow escape from death when a cable was cut and arched across the field where he was working, writhing like a coiled snake with tremendous force. Realising what was happening he raised the alarm. Their vehicles were found but once again they eluded capture. It was getting dangerous when their activities blew the electric transformer in Howden Road cutting off the supply. The farmers were not pleased having to milk by hand as in the old days.

By now they had stolen practically all the accessible copper in the Silsden police section so they moved to new pastures at Gargrave. It was there that tragedy struck as it was bound to do. Electricity can be very dangerous hence the danger warnings on all the poles but these men seemed unafraid of the risks. Had they served their country in wartime they would have been very useful but these thefts were costing the taxpayer a fortune, electricity still being a Nationalised industry or as the Prime Minister Sir Harold said, the family silver!

On their last enterprise one member climbed the ladder with the wire cutters and just as he was about to cut through the copper earth wire the power in the main wires arched and electrocuted him. His comrades took him to Skipton Hospital and left him at the door. Initially it was treated as murder for there was no one to give an explanation but gradually the facts were pieced together for the Inquest. The victim was a young man taken before his time. His death likely prevented other deaths because it brought an end to that type of thieving. Of course for such escapades to be successful there has to be somewhere to dispose of the wire and first it had to be burned off. This was done in secret locations such as on the moor by Robin Hood's stone.

Chapter 35

All for Love

Occasionally I was expected to help train young constables and introduce them to country policing and the well-tried beat system. I would like to think they learned something if only the beauty of Wharfedale and the characters living in it. One young man, we'll call Rory, was courting and on his rest day both decided to come over on the number 12 bus from Haworth to Addingham to enjoy a good hike.

It was August. The weather was hot and sultry but that was never a deterrent to lovers, for such they were. They called at Addingham police office to get into suitable boots then took the footpath through the cricket field to go up to the Addingham Moorside ridge.

Both were in their early twenties and very fit, making good progress up through Overgate croft, then past one or two old mill stones half concealed in the thick bracken on Fothergills and finally onto the high moor. The views of Pendle, Ingleborough Whernside and Pen y Ghent were excellent and during the whole trip up there they hadn't seen a soul. They refreshed themselves at Windy gate Nick where the plane crashed in the war, gazed at the distant Doubler Stones then followed the boundary wall towards Ilkley. I had told Rory the wall was built by two brothers from Halifax and is to their credit. It separates the parish of Addingham from Silsden. When first built old Ernest Todd of Low Mill told me a section of it was built on a bog and if you jumped up and down the wall would move.

The international forestry group planted conifers on the Blackpots Moor side of the wall which ruined the once famous grouse moor but the young couple were not going there on account of the flies. Instead, Rory had previously noticed a snug little hollow surrounded by rocks and high heather; a perfect private place for a picnic!

The heather was in full bloom, the bees and butterflies were working and the scent was heavenly. Rory pondered why I had said, "don't get shot!" as they set off. He was soon to find out!

The young couple enjoyed their feast with a bottle of wine and as it was so warm stripped to the bare necessities, knowing no one knew they were there in this remote, secret place.

They had just nicely snuggled up together when a curlew gave its beautiful but piercing cry from close by.

"That's an alarm note!" said Rory who was a keen ornithologist. "There's probably a fox or a crow about!" He pulled the tartan plaid over them both having noticed a small flight of midges hovered over them attracted by the bare flesh. Once more they settled down.

Then a great commotion occurred when a covey of nine grouse with loud guttural calls of 'go back' planed in and landed all around them unaware of the couple's presence. They peeped out from beneath their canopy admiring this truly British bird with its reddish plumage, its bright red wattle over the eye and its fascinating way of communicating, almost like some ancient language. Then, as if startled, they rose into the air and were gone. "Now, where were we?" said Jane.

Now, as Rory told me on their return, they were just approaching an exalted conclusion when they heard a strange rhythmic swishing sound. It was coming nearer. He left his love to look over the rock parapet and was shocked to see an army of grouse beaters with white flags coming straight for them.

"Quick, love," he ordered, get under the plaid and pretend your asleep we're in the middle of a grouse shoot; I'd forgotten it was the Glorious Twelfth; there's a whole line of 'em heading this way.

The swishing sound got louder and louder then began to fade. Rory cautiously looked out just as the first shots rang out from the line of sunken butts he had failed to notice to their front. He could see the sun reflecting on metal or glass and felt in his rucksack for his binoculars.

"Oh heck," he said, dismayed, "I knew George Oldfield shot somewhere up here. He's in the butt right opposite and he's got a telescope!"

"Who's George Oldfield?" asked Jane in all innocence.

"He's Assistant Chief Constable in charge of CID running the Ripper Enquiry and he knows me!" said Rory just a little concerned.

"We've done nothing wrong," said Jane, "Don't worry!"

"Pack up," said Rory, "Let's go into the woods!"

As they settled among the Scots pines the gunfire faded at last to be replaced by the sound of a redpoll family near their old nest. Peace from the World again. No one told them falling in love could be such a hazardous venture!

One of my police piper friends was Colin the nearest chap to Robert Burns I ever met. We were both in the police pipe band during its ill-fated short life. The problem for my friend was he could not help attracting the opposite sex and he already had one wife. Extramarital activities were frowned on and were frequently punished for 'they had their ways!'

The arrival of a police vehicle outside my home station was common place so I did not look up from my desk until the door opened to admit the most beautiful police woman anyone could wish to see. Tall, smart, pleasing presence and figure and a complexion of peaches and cream what an advert for recruitment I thought. She was followed by Colin. He explained he was teaching this Goddess the bagpipes.

I ushered them into the house and sat them on the settee, then my wife asked if they would like a cup of tea. Up until then the young lady had not spoken and I suppose I was expecting dulcet tones to match her appearance but I was wrong again.

"Aye, love," she said, "That would be right grand but I'd rather have a pint of Barnsley bitter!"

This was said in broad Yorkshire dialect which my wife and I were not expecting. However she was lovely and was excellent company which no doubt was why she was with Colin.

For a while we heard nothing of him then I met a mutual piper friend of Colin who related this tale.

Keen piper Colin had gone on a piping course in a remote little village in the highlands from where he sent a postcard to his section which was pinned on the notice board for all to see. Also arriving at the Section was another postcard from the gorgeous police woman from the same Scottish village with the same time and date on.

Both officers were on the carpet and in spite of the incriminating evidence the Superintendent could not prove they were away together. A great deal was at stake for Colin was a married man and such were the restrictions on personal behaviour he could be punished.

Two months late witness summonses arrived for the pair from Scotland. Seemingly they had witnessed a road accident and were required to give evidence in court. The Superintendent took no pleasure in banishing each of them to the opposite ends of the county for they were both good officers but they had been caught out by their own folly or was it folly. They got at least one more night together when they returned to Scotland to give evidence and no one could do a thing about it!

Out with Rory at Low Mill where thieves had been active near where I found my largest ever Cannabis crop, we noticed a car registered in Manchester.

We entered the derelict garden of the late mill manager. It was a wilderness. The day was not warm but overcast and threatening with rain as we quietly walked down the path Rory close at my heels.

I stopped suddenly and Rory almost collided. Scarcely could I believe my eyes for right in front of us on the ground among all the weeds was a young couple, the young man prone facing heaven and the girl sitting astride him. They were totally engrossed.

I hurriedly removed my helmet and Rory did likewise. Signalling to do an about turn we tip-toed out before they became aware of our presence. As I explained to my young protégé, the effect it could have on their love-life to be disturbed by two burly Bobbies! It could spoil their fun for ever! They never knew nor did I ever break my silence on the young lady whose identity I knew! I just hoped they didn't catch cold!

Chapter 36

Riot Training

During the first miners' strike I was paired up with a road traffic officer and we toured the county checking on the security of power stations and the like. I visited places I had never heard of and was reminded how lucky I was policing in Wharfedale. I did not care for disputes of any kind which was why I joined the police to keep the peace as I had done in the army.

My first industrial dispute was in Baildon and at that time it was the longest running in our history. It was unpleasant at times when the police were not present and quite violent especially at the homes of those workers who could not afford to strike.

On my Cambridge interviews a high-ranking officer asked me what I thought about the trade unions.

I told him that if employers looked after their work force properly there would be no need for trade unions. He nodded in agreement so I continued. From what I see, loyal workers are often treated very badly which makes strong trade unions essential. I added that I had never belonged to a trade union having worked for the aristocracy and whilst some such employers were excellent as one would expect from the ruling classes, others were a disgrace and seemed to delight in paying low wages and failing to maintain agricultural housing whilst living a lavish lifestyle. It is that sort of thing that leads to disputes and an unhappy populace and, if left unattended, to revolution as history has shown.

After the defeat of the Heath government my own force began regular riot training or 'trudging and wedging' as it was called. We used tactics that were used by the Greeks and Romans. They were very physical and very intimidating to those on the wrong side of the shields and when batons were rhythmically beaten on the front of the shields as we advanced I imagine it would have instilled some fear into those we were trying to dislodge. It was sad really for I suspected who the victims were going to be; men who for generations had laboured underground for private employers who had not always played the game leading to Nationalisation after the war; men who were now pawns in a game of chess and going to get a bloody nose for bringing down a government; men who had kept our industries going in two world wars. It is so convenient to forget.

Part of the training was the large numbers of officers would be split in two, one official police the other rioters throwing bricks and fire at us. It was heavy going and some of those men were clearly not up to it. One curious thing noticed by others of us who had served in the military, those training officers could have been straight off the parade ground shouting orders like we were a bunch of learner rookies instead of experienced officers of the Crown.

At the break time I reminded some of my colleagues that I was engaged in riot drill at the age of 18. We called it IS or Internal Security drill. We wore kilt boots and puttees, battledress, ammo pouches and a steel helmet. We carried a Lee Enfield rifle with ten rounds in the magazine and a bayonet of Sheffield steel at the end of the barrel. We would have obeyed orders, but all this choreography was for rioting insurgents in far outposts of a fading empire not our own people who lived and worked alongside us who might belong to a trade union or a different political party!

As a parting shot I said how do they know which side of the barricades some of us will be on if the balloon really goes up? For me I was in some pain having injured my back in the winter and still wonder, was it my back or the comments I made but I never went on any more riot training. Perhaps someone overheard! Seriously, I had a premonition of what was going to happen and what it would do to the police force in the long term. I think we have all had time to digest that now. The police force is very different from the days before the second miners' strike and although all our people are the losers it's the ordinary folks who are the biggest losers of all.

I recall, as Christmas approached during my first year in the village bottles of wine, biscuits, sherry etc. started to appear behind the police office counter from which three of us worked. I was told by Norman the senior constable that they were gifts from the five licensees to each of us; that it was a tradition. I had reservations about this practice no matter how long it had been in existence and made it clear I wanted no part of it whatever.

My pile of presents continued to mount so on the first day duty I put them all in a bag hidden under my cape and went round each of the licensed premises. I had a mixed reception. Some took them back grudgingly but Pat at the Swan said she admired me for it but really would like me to have the present. I told her I would when she gave every customer she had a free bottle of sherry at Christmas pointing out I must be free to enforce the licencing laws without fear or favour. She understood but some were a little bit wary of me after that but at least I could sleep easily. After all, I did not drink in any public house locally and I knew a large percentage of troubles caused in families and with crime generally were caused by alcohol.

A manager of one of the factories approached me about a matter and in the course of the conversation said 'every man has his price'! To that I said maybe but in the case of this man the price would be far too high. Then to drive the point home I told him if I was offered a bribe I would take it with my left hand and with my right hand I would take the person into custody. I think he understood.

The famous cricketer Freddie Trueman frequented the Swan public house in those days. Long after, a former Addingham resident saw me waiting for the bus.

"It's P.C.Pickles isn't it?"

"Not any more it isn't," I replied.

He informed me he used to drink at the Swan and how they would send someone out to see where I was before leaving, they were so afraid of being breathalysed. Always I carried a kit in my tunic pocket. I told him I was pleased to hear that for between us we might have prevented an accident or too or even saved lives!

One night just before Christmas, I checked the Co-op store near my home before going off duty. It was after 1.0 a.m. As I went into the small yard at the rear I heard a sound in the pitch dark. Switching on my torch I saw there was a man just in front of me. He said he was urinating but there was no sign of that. Looking him up and down I saw he was wearing two pairs of trousers such as a climber might wear. Near him was the drain-pipe leading up near the loading bay. He could give no reasonable explanation and declined to tell me where he was from so I arrested him. There was a van on the Crown car park with a number of men inside but they hadn't seen me and the prisoner.

I needed assistance but we had no radios then and all I could do was to quietly knock on the pub door for I knew there would be a few regulars in there still drinking. I explained the position and two burly locals who knew me well came to help whilst the licensee sent for reinforcements from Skipton.

They were a gang of burglars in possession of every type of implement a serious burglar would wish for. They were from South Yorkshire, all out of work miners, trying to bring something home for Christmas. The court took this into account.

A likeable rogue, a former Irish Guardsman who sailed near the wind a bit too often stole some tools and I found them in his van. To everyone's amazement he admitted it and took his punishment well. His list was fascinating for one in such an illustrious regiment and clearly he was leading a charmed life. One thing after another he was a suspect but nothing could be proved then, to cock a snook at the system he was drinking in Otley and missed the bus. One bus remained in the bus station, the engine ticking over and no driver in sight. The opportunity was there and he took it and drove home leaving the double decker carefully parked on the council estate just a stone's throw from his home. As usual, nothing could be proved but the village had a laugh at his audacity!

Chapter 37

The Exhumation

As children we were brought up to respect the dead; never to walk over or remove anything from a grave. To desecrate a grave was a serious offence. The dead had to be left in peace and bad luck would befall those who disturbed them!

When I was instructed to attend an exhumation at Bolton Priory I went with mixed feelings and as the day wore on my anxieties intensified.

An elderly group of academic types with a supposed archaeological interest had obtained a Home Office licence to exhume a grave, in legend the grave of Lord John Clifford killed at Ferrybridge a preliminary to the battle of Towton and buried beneath a large stone in the grounds of the ruined Augustinian Priory.

Part of the legend indicated the Cliffords were buried standing up so that on the day of Judgement they were ready for off when the trumpets sounded. The men and women in this team wished to establish if it was the grave of the Clifford and if he was in fact upstanding. To me it seemed a frivolous reason to be disturbing such a grave of a brave man who had been at peace for hundreds of years and there is nowhere more peaceful than Bolton Priory most of the time!

The group also had written permission from the Duke of Devonshire's estate. I was there because it was a rare thing for this to happen and because the Home Office controlled the police and did not easily permit exhumations.

I had doubts about the venture from the start when I saw they had no strong men with them to move the stone. Nor did they seem to have adequate tools. When I noticed a fellow visiting them from a Civil War enactment society I became more concerned but they had all the necessary papers so I had no legal right to intervene.

When it came to pull the stone away with a rope the group had insufficient strength to do it so the Guardian newspaper reporter and myself were literally roped in to assist. Once the stone was off the elderly archaeologists began to use their trowels in the age old way which was very proper and slow.

There was great excitement when they encountered human bones but the two skeletons they found were lying prone and were both female! There was no sign of The Clifford or any artefacts, just the bones of two unknown ladies disturbed for vanity!

The Augustinians blended in well with the local population therefore there should be no raised eyebrows on the burial of ladies in an all-male establishment!

Some years after an article in the newspaper was brought to my notice. It covered the day of the exhumation and claimed everyone who took part suffered a nervous breakdown. If it is true it reinforces my long-held beliefs that the dead should not be disturbed yet television programmes delight in digging people up on the slightest pretext of furthering science or is it sensationalism and idle curiosity.

Worship at Addingham has taken place since Saxon times and from the number of graves in the church yard our people have been buried here since those times. Like Bolton Priory it is a peaceful place, if a little crowded when a new grave is required. The late Harry Ridley dug many graves in his time assisted by others and because of the ancient history of the place it is not surprising when digging a grave, when surplus soil is thrown down the bank towards the river, that some human remains should find their way down there as well.

This first came to light with me when a fisherman called David Brown brought a human skull to my office. He found it in shallow water below the graveyard. We had it reinterred without fuss for it was clearly very old.

Shortly after that a real fuss broke out when two young lads from Keighley started coming over to fish the Wharfe. Fishing became secondary to their archaeological finds for each time they came they recovered human bones and took them home, each with his share, secretly hidden in cardboard boxes beneath their beds. The big thigh bones were the most difficult to hide on the bus over Cringles but they got away with it almost until they each had a near complete skeleton then one of the mothers found her son's treasure and nearly died herself. His pal's hoard was exposed and the cat was really out of the bag.

All the bones were returned to the church and reinterred by the Rev. Shaw without fuss or publicity.

Digging in the garden next door to Addingham police office I unearthed sections of hazel still with the cut marks and clumps of recognisable heather. This was found in strange peat-like soil. The hazel was from wattle and the heather from thatch. I also found bones and pottery so abandoned the digging and informed the museums department at Ilkley. They did a controlled excavation and cited the bones I had found as human, red deer, oxen, and cat. The pottery was mostly Anglo-Saxon with some Roman. They concluded the site was part of the ancient site of the Anglo-Saxon village before the Norman invasion.

Mr Job Brear of the saw mill told me the heather grew all the way down from the Moorside to the railway line. He stood with me watching Ogden demolition team dismantling the railway bridge over Main Street. On it was written 'Vote for Brear'. He told me he had been present when the first stone was laid to build the bridge. He lived to be two weeks short of one hundred and two.

I kept bees at the saw mill, the hives on a site that he and his brother kept bees in Queen Victoria's reign. They liked to wager and one scheme was to put a number of bees' in different paper bags with some white flour and after marking the hive one of them crossed the river and went up the beacon and at a certain time the bees were released while the other brother waited with a stop watch at the hives. The bees' first back at the hive meant the winner was the owner of that hive. I suppose it was a simple way of something to do.

A swarm of bees at Ben Rhydding was causing a problem to passers-by. The swarm had been hanging in a privet bush over the pavement for some time and consequently were hungry and bad tempered and stingy. As no one else was available I was asked to remove them.

I got the swarm into a cardboard box and thought I had secured it but setting off back to Addingham they began to escape. To have large numbers of angry bees flying about inside a vehicle is disconcerting so I drove to Ilkley Police station hoping to borrow an old sheet with which to enclose them. The only thing available was the large union flag lying freshly laundered and neatly folded on the desk. Grabbing this I ran back to the vehicle and quickly wrapped it round the box then ran with it like it was explosive, which it was, to the derelict garden at the back of the station. Then I sprayed the box with water from the hose pipe to calm them which it did.

Badly stung, I sat on the step out of sight counting thirty-five stings on one leg, plus others all over my body, especially the unprotected head and face. I felt rotten but the bees were settling and I resolved to leave them in situ until housed in a proper hive when I would remove them to Addingham.

I noticed Chief Inspector Hardy cautiously looking round the corner of the building. He was aware what I was engaged in but had not expected to see so many angry bees whizzing about. He departed hurriedly. Some people are afraid of bees! Had the bees not been removed they might have stung some other poor person and my pain might have been there's. This sort of activity was quite common in the summer months but the secret is, if one suspects the bees have been hanging several days, to let a member of the local beekeepers association deal with it, armed with plenty of antihistamine!

Frank was a keen beekeeper and because of that common interest became a friend. He was an interesting man, a chemist by profession but during the war was among that brave band of commandoes fighting the Nazis in Crete. After the war he continued with his chemical business at Ilkley where he made a grave error in the storage of containers containing a dangerous chemical which leaked and caused death. Frank went to prison for manslaughter. Sympathetic members of the beekeeping fraternity cared for his bees until his release. Frank continued to return to Crete where he even kept a hive of bees producing excellent honey tasting of thyme. I suppose his regular return was to honour his comrades who were still lying out there.

One day at a meeting at Ilkley Frank asked to speak to me privately. What he said was alarming and so strange that I was only half convinced .Firstly he said he came to me because of all the coppers he knew I was the only one he trusted. He went on to say two men he shared a business with had threatened to kill him. They were both chemists like him and they had made an amazing discovery – how to run motor vehicles on water! He assured me this was true but they had fallen out hence the threats which he said were very real.

All this was said in an adjoining room where the everyday stories of beekeeping were being discussed and at the time, I confess, it seemed too incredible!

A fortnight later Frank called at my home station and gave me a typed piece of paper with the names and details of the two men he alleged were going to kill him. I placed the document in a locked drawer just in case what he was saying was true. As he left he said "If anything happens to me in the next two weeks you know who to look for!" I assured him it would be investigated.

Some ten days after I was collecting correspondence at Ilkley police station when the phone was answered by the duty officer. I heard Frank's name mentioned and was told his wife had just found him dead. Talk about shivers down the spine!

I contacted CID told them the story and asked them to treat the death as suspicious. I didn't think they believed the story and I suppose, who could blame them. The post mortem revealed death by natural causes and that was the end of the matter but who is better qualified than a chemist, other than a medical practitioner, to taking life and making it look natural?

I contacted Frank's solicitor who knew something of Frank's fears. He said he knew about the discovery and the dispute and that the two men had very good reason to get rid of Frank but there was little any one could do about it. If the discovery were true it would have been worth a King's Ransom for the oil companies would likely have silenced it at any price.

Some of us will always wonder what the truth really was but sometimes it is difficult to stir people into action when something a little out of the ordinary comes along, especially when it means complicated enquiries. I did not let him down but did the system?

Scene of Exumation

River Wharfe and pool below bridge and stepping stones where unfortunate drowning casualties were sometimes washed down from the dangerous Strid.

Chapter 38

Murder

Between Lob Wood and the water extraction plant near the ancient Saxon boundary of Addingham and Bolton Abbey, is a rough piece of woodland alongside the River Wharfe. People do not generally walk in there because it is dangerous. One morning, a young man on leave from his veterinary studies at Edinburgh University did walk through that rough area. He lived at Storriths where his grandfather had been a gamekeeper and his father another employee of the Bolton Abbey estate. The young man was also a born naturalist and knew one saw little of interest on footpaths which was why he chose the wood.

By pure chance he stumbled on the body of a man lying on his back fully clothed and still warm. He quickly reported the matter to the police. Senior officers, CID; just about everyone descended on the place but decided not to touch the body until the arrival of the Home Office Pathologist Dr. Gee. Some officers thought it a 'hit and run' that the body had been thrown over the wall in haste. Others thought, rightly that it was foul play but we had to wait for the pathologist and we waited a long time. The West Riding liked to take its time!

However, when the great man arrived and the body was turned over he had a screw driver in his back. It transpired he was a debt collector from Lancashire, always a dangerous job when dealing with desperate people. As soon as this was known practically everyone melted away and a humble P.C. was left to arrange the removal of the body, fix up a post mortem and deal with the death. CID would deal with the murder enquiry.

It was fortuitous that Mr. Nelson walked through that area of rough woodland. Had he not done so the body might never have been found or at least not for a long time instead of on the very morning it had been left while still warm!

The murderer was arrested soon after and sentenced to life imprisonment.

A report from Addingham Moorside of a cow bellowing in distress in the middle of a field led me to witness a very sad scene. The cow had calved, assisted by the old farmer who had used a cow tie to pull the calf out. The calf was dead and so was the old farmer. The exertion must have been too much for his heart and there he was lying alongside the dead calf still holding the cow tie and the bereft cow bellowing for its lost calf.

Whilst on foot patrol in the Moorside lane I decided to stop the next vehicle for a routine check. There was a male driver in the vehicle and papers stuck to the windscreen indicated he had just come through customs at an east coast port. He told me he had been to Holland and was on his way to Liverpool. I obtained all his details and examined his documents, making notes, for there was just something about him that did not ring true then I allowed him to proceed.

I put in a short intelligence report and very quickly received a call from Interpol. This was the first siting of this man for a number of years after he jumped ship in Cape Town. He was wanted for a number of offences including drug dealing. They were glad of the information and able to resume their enquiries. Had I not gone to investigate a number of dead pigs dumped by an inconsiderate farmer in a small quarry at Four Lane Ends I would not have been in the right place at the right time!

An amusing incident began at Four Lane Ends by Straight Lane when I was on foot yet again .A large white van was cruising along from Silsden in a suspicious manner and rightly, I suspected poaching. As the driver crossed the junction heading down towards Ilkley I signalled him to stop but he ignored the sign and accelerated away. At that moment I was the only person in sight but within seconds a mini came along containing a young couple who knew me. I waved them down, explained the position, and we went after the white van. I think they quite enjoyed the chase. We followed at a distance to Farfield where we overtook them with me crouched out of sight. Just before Bolton Bridge I got out, thanked the couple and sent them off.

When the van came into view I stood in the road ready to bolt should he decide to run me over but he stopped. As I thought they were travellers on a poaching spree. Two lurchers lay in the back of the van along with gate nets but no dead hares or other game.

The driver's face and that of the boy beside him was a picture for they had seen me shortly before two miles away when they thought they had escaped my notice yet here I was again at Bolton Bridge with no sign of how I arrived there. Perhaps they thought I had wings! Dealing with such people for minor offences was always a difficulty and in this case not worth the effort. Travellers were here today and gone tomorrow and not easy to trace even for serious offences. They promised to keep away from Wharfedale! Certainly I never saw that band here again; perhaps it was the apparent supernatural uniformed Bobbie springing from one side of the valley to the other! Who knows!

The winters were very harsh with heavy falls of snow and severe frosts. Outlying farms were often cut off for a few days and livestock could go hungry. Up the Roman Road at Addingham lived three spinster sisters, Lucy, Margaret and Edith. When their parents were alive they walked each day to work in the mill at Silsden but now they ran the farm. Unable to raise them on the telephone and to make sure they were alright I walked up. The road was well drifted in which required a bit of negotiating at times but eventually I reached the farm. The door was open but no sign of life then I heard voices and discovered the three of them further along the Roman Road in the ditch with a large milk churn. The water at the farm was frozen and the small spring in the ditch was the only running water available for their animals. So there they were ladling a panful at a time into the large churn then Lucy, the strongest of the three, carried the churn on her back the couple of hundred yards to the farm.

All three were dressed in multiple old clothing held together with binder twine. They had bright red weather beaten faces and red chapped hands. Only in Russia would I have expected to see such a scene yet they were cheerful; pleased to see me and glad of my concern. This was their way of life and they saw no reason to change it.

Chapter 39

Mods and Rockers

From time to time cults develop with the young. Always there have been gangs, a throwback to when we all lived as clans or tribes. It's in our genes manifesting its- self when I was soldiering, trying to prop up the fading empire when Sir Winston Churchill was prime minister whilst many of my age group were playing at being 'Teddy Boys'. Like other gangs before them they were not always harmless. There we were ready to give our lives for our country when thugs and bullies were spoiling things at home! There were National Service soldiers who felt the Teds should be put up against a wall and shot but of course that was not British so the poor old Bobbies had to deal with their activities every weekend for as long as the fad lasted.

Then came the 'Mods and Rockers' another cult dressed in Crombie coats and long parkas drawing attention by using threatening behaviour. They travelled in packs and caused problems for the public and the police who tried to keep them in order.

One regimental sergeant major I knew would have loved to have drilled them on the square for an hour or two and felt, with the aid of his training instructors, he could have made some use of them. As he said, "their fathers rose to the occasion when war threatened and acquitted themselves admirably." One of his sergeants thought they should all be disposed of quietly without suffering somewhere in the Irish Sea as food for the crabs and lobsters. Perhaps the sergeant could be forgiven for his intolerance for he had been one of the first into Belsen Concentration Camp in 1945 and it distressed him greatly to see young Britons squandering their birth right by making law-abiding people afraid.

The first hint of trouble came as I sat in my arm chair in my home station having just gone off duty. A chanting sound came from up the village and was getting louder like the racket one got at a football match. Cars were stopping in the street and then there appeared a large band of fifty plus young men all in black wearing Crombie coats marching like the 'Black Shirts' of the 1930s. They started rocking a car outside the police office, trying to turn it over. I asked my wife to ring for help, threw on a tweed jacket and pushed my staff up my sleeve.

I followed at a distance as they progressed towards Ilkley full of bravado and recklessness, forcing cars to swerve or stop and no doubt terrifying some of the occupants. At last they paused at Cornerstones where the bus route was, no doubt hoping for a ride to Ilkley, it being open country now with no one to terrorise. It was then a dog handler arrived with 'Sparky' a fierce Alsatian who had an excellent reputation for dealing with naughty people. Also, two road traffic police arrived. It was then the mob turned their attention on us.

Some of the ringleaders were screaming "Kill the pigs" and the situation was looking very ugly. I drew my staff and advised the other officers to do the same and to concentrate on the ringleaders. We then charged at them expecting a difficult fight being sorely outnumbered but many ran away immediately, screaming like stuck pigs. Some, desperate to escape jumped over the high wall into Hall Croft; others were taken screaming and struggling to the police car. There was a limit on the number of prisoners we could take with just the one car. We could hardly have thrown them in with Sparky for he would have eaten them; he had tasted one or two and clearly enjoyed it.

The ringleaders arrested the rest of the mob huddled together, sullen and resentful, much like all prisoners of war do. There was still over fifty, all from Keighley and Silsden, so we organised a bus to take them to where they belonged under a police escort. We were not equipped to deal with such a bunch and were glad to see the back of them.

There was no repeat of this type of disorder locally and as every skirmish needs a hero ours was the faithful police dog Sparky who helped put the enemy to flight and had a light meal doing it.

The five public houses in the village had always been very law abiding.

The police enforced the Licensing laws which were very strict and required our presence on a regular basis just to show the flag.

Some wives would complain about after hours drinking especially on pay day when the husband would return home with a light pay packet. We always gave the licensee a chance to take his own action with a warning of what could happen.

The licensee after Sandy Gunn at the Craven Heifer altered the pub dramatically and encouraged a new clientele of young people, mostly from outside the village. It became so popular that there was scarcely room to move as the evening advanced and the Fire Officer was concerned for the safety of the customers should anything untoward arise.

On receiving a request of help from the licensee dealing with a drunken customer a colleague and I went to assist.

Customers were so numerous they were blocking the entrance at the front and the exit at the rear but slowly, trying not to alarm the revellers; we got to the bar and confronted the young man causing the problem. He was about twenty and it was whispered to us he was a professional boxer with convictions for causing grievous bodily harm. He was asked to leave by the licensee and seemed reasonable enough at that stage but once out in the small yard at the rear he became very aggressive and knocked my colleague, an ex-Coldstream Guardsman due to retire from the police, through a window.

A crowd of his cronies were round him by now egging him on and pulling the hair of my colleague and there developed a very unpleasant tussle with me wrestling him to the ground to handcuff him. To their credit, other customers came to our aid and helped to get the cuffs on. Our assailants were not only young men but young women too and my colleague managed to lock a number of them in an outhouse but not before they had thrown his helmet and radio.

We had nicely got control taking names and addresses of those we were going to prosecute when an Inspector arrived from Keighley. He also was a famous ex-Royal Marine boxer and was just a little annoyed that one of his old comrades had been so roughly dealt with. As we escorted the drunken prisoner towards the police car the Inspector upbraided him for his stupid behaviour. The fellow had drunk a full bottle of pernod. We sat him in the rear seat. In front of him, lying over the passenger seat was the brand new raincoat of the Inspector. The prisoner, once he sat comfortably in the warmth of the vehicle was violently sick over the new coat. So much for upbraiding a drunken prisoner!

Amazingly they all pleaded guilty at Skipton Magistrates Court but there was as yet another minor episode concerning that pub where, until the current licensee, there had never been a hint of trouble.

Whilst going about my affairs of patrolling that corner of the beat I had to pass the pub. The chap who had shown his dislike of the police already uttered verbal abuse at me which was not acceptable and he was duly reported under the Public Order Act for insulting words or behaviour and a Breach of the Queen's Peace. There was no further trouble.

Down the street from the pub was Ivy House Farm where lived Freddie and Olive Blaythorne. Opposite their home there lived a young couple with a small baby. Like many young couples they had frequent rows and on this occasion both stormed out of the house leaving the door open. Olive witnessing this and out of concern for their baby went across to see if all was well. It was not. An open fire blazed in the grate and the baby was crying and apparently abandoned. Being a kind-hearted person she went looking for the couple and not finding them brought their baby down to me. Well, I had to receive it but never was its grandmother called so quickly to take charge. Now had it been a ferret I would likely have coped better!

Chapter 40

The Fleece

The reorganisation of the Police Force in the 70s and the merging of city and borough forces into one large Metropolitan Force was probably the beginning of the end for Village policing. The County men lived and worked with the people they served in tied houses. City and Borough men tended to live remote from their place of work in their own houses for which they received an allowance. With the steep rise in house prices, those County men living in police accommodation were at a serious disadvantage when the time came for them to buy their own house. There was a list of officers but, often when it came to someone's turn to purchase, the delay had cost them thousands. Just something else we had to take in our stride along with not getting into debt!

In the case of rural men this closeness operated in two ways, namely it kept the Bobby on the straight and narrow in his handling of his people and it encouraged his people to behave because of his continued presence. For him it was a sort of a tightrope unlike his city counterpart who was largely anonymous. Altogether they were a different breed. They tended to promote their former cadets who had come straight from grammar school, having been deferred military service and knowing little of life outside the police. They were a courser or rougher breed and this stood out in their dealings with the public. In one city a group of police officers threw a coloured man into the canal for a lark and he drowned. Fortunately one of the culprits had a conscience.

The Fleece public house was the most popular in the village on music night when people came from great distances to enjoy the guests of John Marsland Heap MBE the licensee for over 20 years and his wife Barbara. During the war John had served in the merchant navy when his ship, the Corbisbay was torpedoed by a U Boat in the Indian Ocean and sank. John saved a number of lives that day and having got onto a life raft some twenty of the crew were adrift in the sea for weeks before they were rescued. Only three survived. For his part in saving the lives of the men he was awarded the equivalent of the Victoria Cross by Lloyds for gallantry.

On John's retirement, David Harrison, an accomplished musician, a good singer and comedian became the licensee aided by his wife Janet. From their music David and his pal David Hopton raised a great deal for various charities. There never was any trouble at the Fleece and the clientele were what could only be described as up-market, especially the local ones living in the village which had changed dramatically since the 60s.

Busy pubs are always a little difficult to clear after a good music session and licensees are loath to offend their regulars on whom their income really depends so inevitably at closing time, being a civilised establishment there is no pressure though the bell has rung.

The law allows a licensee to entertain bone fide friends and guests after hours which can lead a person unfamiliar with local custom to form the wrong idea. An ambitious young Inspector from a former city force came over from Keighley towards pub closing time, expressing a serious interest in the Fleece and Mr. Harrison's customers. So keen was the Inspector that he stood on the wooden commemorative seat beneath the window of the premises. This afforded a good view of the interior and from what he saw he made up his mind to enter the premises despite my cautionary advice.

I knew the law as well as anyone and I could foresee a failed case with embarrassment for the police and the danger of making after hours drinking worse than it was. After all, these were law-abiding people, several professionals, some with sons and daughters in the police and likely the odd police officer in there. What was for certain they supported the police and would always assist and come to our aid. Having lived with these people for nearly twenty years, sharing their triumphs and disasters I did know what I was talking about. In any case it was proposed to change the licensing laws and do away with this outdated farcical loophole in the law so why risk years of goodwill for a case that would surely fail. In all the years other senior officers had invariably accepted my advice and were glad to.

There was a frosty silence the moment we entered the bar. They had also been watching us and knew what to expect. Samples of drink were taken and labelled and the licensee reported for permitting drinking after hours.

In court all the charges were dismissed and the police were made to look just a bit silly and the Fleece carried on as before! Nothing useful was gained except the hardened drinkers had a few laughs at the police expense.

The keen officer who accompanied me that night, on another occasion, was travelling from Silsden to Addingham when he came across a road accident just up from the Craven Heifer where a young schoolgirl had been knocked down and seriously injured. His keenness and speed of action undoubtedly saved her life. It was a long recovery but now grown with children of her own I think of him and hope the good Lord excused him for any minor errors in his service for we all make them!

Coming down past the Fleece one night I came across a badly injured cat lying on the pavement. It had been knocked down by a vehicle, suffering a broken back which had paralysed it. I knew the cat belonged an old lady neighbour of mine. There was no hope of getting a vet out in the middle of the night for a cat so I called in home, collected my rifle with the sound moderator and put the poor cat out of its misery, telling the owner the next day what I had done and where the cat was buried. This action was required from time to time to avert suffering and no doubt it saved the taxpayer a little in call outs for vets. This cat was beyond saving.

A practice had been creeping in when a cow died suddenly and the farmer reporting it to his vet, that the vet, without visiting the farm and examining the cow, would tell the farmer to report it to the police that it was a case of suspect anthrax. This meant the taxpayer paid for the vets visit instead of the farmer. Anthrax was a rare disease and such cows nearly always died from some common ailment.

I broached the subject with a particular vet making him very angry with me for some reason but there were no more casual reporting's of suspected anthrax without a proper vet examination being carried out before the police were informed. I suppose it was one way of saving the farmer a bob or two but it wasn't right and not even vets are above the law. I suppose no one really likes to be found out causing them to vent their spleen on the Bobbie, not a wise thing to do, even with a 'professional'!

Being a rural station meant people bringing in wounded birds and animals quite regularly, often when I had little time to deal with them. A good friend and keen naturalist, Mrs Jean Clapham and her husband Gerald of Potters Hall, came to the rescue by taking in all such casualties and releasing to the wild those which survived.

Duncan Irving of Farfield Farm brought me a kestrel with a broken wing. I took it to a vet I knew in Keighley called Donald Campbell and he splinted it for which I paid ten shillings. Donald was from the island of Tiree and on our first meeting I addressed him in Gaelic. He was very impressed. We would meet for piping practice from time to time at his home. His son Alistair was but a schoolboy in short trousers and one would hardly have believed what the future held for him.

The kestrel, alas did not survive after falling into a bucket of water and drowning. We couldn't win them all!

Jean's father was the celebrated inventor, engineer and motor cyclist William Bradley who lived to a great age. When young his fame began by riding Brough and Scott motor cycles up very steep hills round about the dales. It was quite a cult in those days. He was thought of as a genius by some and when Betty's Café was wrecked by an explosion one night he quickly calculated in his head the pressure the boiler must have been under that cold and frosty night to send pieces sailing through the roof and damaging other property. Initially, the police thought it was the work of the I.R.A. very active at that time.

Farmer's wife, Joyce Irving informed me she had found a badger in a snare in Lob Wood adjoining their land. As badgers were then protected by law I went along and invited Mrs Clapham to come with me. Having heard barn owls were back nesting in the nearby barn we went to have a look. One owl flew out of an upper window and as we stood talking the hay in the loft above started to move and out crawled a slightly embarrassed couple who I recognised. They said a sheepish hello and slipped away hand in hand. Well, it was springtime and that's what we expected the young Addinghamites to do!

We found where the badger had been strangled in the snare but both had gone, collected by the trapper. I had my suspicions but knew the protection of wild creatures was not an easy task but there were other ways of skinning a cat!

Steel sprung gin traps had been illegal since 1958 but in remote places they were still used. The head mistresses cat went missing and she felt a certain youth was responsible. Sure enough the cat was found in a gin trap caught by its leg. These traps were extremely cruel and were rightly outlawed. As a boy I trapped my hand in one concealed and set to catch a fox. I learned about the pain animals suffered!

Gamekeepers had been the main users of gin traps yet it was a gamekeeper who came with a complaint of a farm worker setting them to catch his pheasants out in the open. This was extremely reckless as any bird or animal including a dog might have been caught. The magistrates took a dim view of the practice.

Chapter 41

The Gala

In the 60s, Addingham Gala was one of the highlights of the year involving all sections of the community. It helped to bring people together whether from the four churches or those who did not subscribe to religious beliefs. The children loved the preparation, the dressing up and on the day, the floats and bands. John Lodge never failed to enter in some fancy costume and Di Wallbank and Jean Birch took control of the floats.

The parade usually started off at the Green led by Jimmy Hadley from the Parish Council followed by the City of Bradford or the Police Pipe Band and slowly meandered down Main Street to the Gala Field on Bolton Road. Amazingly the main trunk road was not closed for this event and vehicles were expected to pull in and allow the floats to pass when they met on bends such as the Sailor or the post office. A constable would also be at the front to see the traffic behaved. It was a jolly affair which really did unify the village.

On one such occasion the builder Jack Clay came for a chat. He was very proud of his achievements in the building trade and told me there were three ways a man got on: one was if he inherited wealth, the other was if he was given help and the third was if he cheated. I suppose that was about right! Jack had been my grandparents' milk boy when he came from Lancashire to work on the farm near Thwaites, Keighley so he had done extremely well. Like my great grandmother he could neither read nor write but that did not hold back his ambition nor did it seem to impede her though she never once used a telephone or travelled in a motor vehicle but spoke reasonable English and excellent Gaelic!

On Gala night there was a dance held in the Memorial Hall and it was well attended by locals with a sprinkling from outside the parish, usually Silsden or Skipton. In those days the allegiance of the village was to Skipton as it had been since Norman times. From a Police point of view Ilkley might as well have been in Russia such was the lack of contact with that town even though we were all part of the West Riding Constabulary.

Just in case of trouble PC Lister and I kept an eye on things. As always it is the drink and sometimes a falling out over a girl that starts the trouble and so it was my first night of Addingham Gala Dance between eleven and midnight, a dangerous time. A fight started in the main hall and spread to the entrance lobby. Unfortunately the exit doors did not open outward and many people were trapped against the glass or lying against the doors on the floor. With the assistance of the stewards, local shopkeepers and councillors', PC Lister and I gained access. For a short time it was very rough and there were a few swollen faces then, as they sobered up, a few red faces. A number of local men were taken before Skipton court and other local men were glad to give evidence against them for spoiling the dance. Des Birch, Jack Dixon, Mr Adams and P.C. Norman Lister acquitted themselves very well.

As the years went by this sort of behaviour became a thing of the past. Once potential troublemakers are made aware it will not only cost them in their pocket but also in their reputation's they generally think again which is as it should be. The threat of humiliation is a much underestimated deterrent!

I have mentioned P.C. L before, the soldier who fought in Korea with the United Nations, who killed a savage dog and was posted to Keighley, who 'smacked' an inspector who insulted him and was posted to a much more salubrious beat at Burley; who had to be restrained by fellow officers when being insulted by a mob at a big demonstration. Here's a little more about this useful asset to the Police Force.

P.C. L had called into Ilkley Police station to collect some correspondence and was standing in front of the fireplace. An attractive young lady came in to produce her driving documents at the desk and was being attended to by the office man. The lady listened fascinated to the conversation of P.C. L and Sergeant Chapman.

Now P.C. L's lowland Scots accent contained many ripe and pointed expletives which would not be acceptable in any company except those from Glasgow, Coatbridge or Stirling. He couldn't help it; that was the way he was. As he went into the back room the lady said how wonderful it was to hear a Scot speaking in the Gaelic language. Well, P.C. L did not speak Gaelic but we knew what she meant and were glad that she had not understood a word of what he had said!

Accompanied by P.C. Pitt, P.C. L visited the home of an elderly spinster lady in the town where a supposed burglary had taken place but nothing stolen. The two officers quickly realised the lady was a wee bit eccentric and that there was no evidence of a burglary. She then took them to a bedroom window facing the moor where she pointed to the putty in the window casing which the bluetits had been pecking. The lady was not convinced so the officer tried a different tack. "It's the curlews love; they come down off the moor at night and peck the putty out; they have the long beaks and they're good at it. It's not a burglary; it's just the curlews!" The lady seemed to like the idea that such big birds were visiting her bedroom window at night and thanked the officers for solving the problem.

A moment of glory for Ilkley Police came when two rival gangs arrived by bus and train one afternoon to do battle with each other in the picturesque peaceful town. Three duty officers rushed to the railway station. There was P.C. L, former Black Watch, P.C. Pitt, former Coldstream Guards and 'Big John' another ex-serviceman.

The gangs were armed with many types of weapon, some had knives, staves, machetes, and chains and clubs various! Three officers somehow rounded up some thirty men, ordered them into three ranks and still armed prepared to march them to the Police Station. P.C. L was in his element; this was what he'd been trained for as a peace keeper. He addressed them all very loudly in his pronounced Scottish accent so that all might hear:

"Right, you bastards, you will march to the time I call out and if any one of you breaks ranks I'll smash his f…ing skull, do you understand?" The mob murmured a reply. "Remember, the first to break ranks will never be the same even if the rest of yous escape, which you won't. Now quick march, right wheel; left right, left right, left right." The amazing thing they obeyed to the entertainment of those townsfolk who were there.

As obedient as a cadre of squaddies they were paraded along the Grove and up Riddings Road to halt outside the Police Station. The office man disarmed them at the gate as they entered the old Victorian Building to be searched properly and placed in the now inadequate cells, or Trap One, and Two as they were called. A large pile of weapons was gathered together for evidence of an affray and when further reinforcements arrived from Keighley the gangs were processed and charged. For their efforts the men received commendations from the Chief Constable and big John was promoted Sergeant.

There is no doubt the prompt action by those officers prevented perhaps the biggest disturbance Ilkley would have endured and no violence was used and no one was injured. Discipline mixed with a little psychology and animal cunning born of experience of men was all that was required and that day Ilkley had the right mix!

Perhaps the climax of P.C. L's career occurred on a day when two young boys were playing on an island in the river Wharfe near Burley-in-Wharfedale unaware that in the higher reaches of the valley it was raining hard and the river was rising. It is said the Wharfe is the fastest rising river in Britain. The boys quickly became marooned and a passer-by reported it to the Police. P.C L and P.C. Whalley, the Burley Bobbies ran across the fields to find the boys in terrible peril from the rising waters.

P.C. L was a swimming instructor and was very strong. Without hesitation, regardless for his own safety, he plunged into the torrent now shoulder high; struggling through the fierce current to reach the boys now petrified; barely hanging onto willow branches. Placing one under each arm he held onto a stout willow trunk and prayed the Fire Service would soon arrive for he knew he could not make the return journey to the bank. He held the heads of the boys as high as he could but already the water was up to his chin and the pressure of the current was overbearing. To his horror one of the boys was torn from his grasp and carried away downstream.

The Fire Brigade arrived at last and PC L and the one boy were saved; sadly the other drowned. Later this greatly affected PC L.

P.C. L and P.C. Whalley received Life-Saving awards for their gallant attempt saving life.

Years later, talking to PC L, he disclosed he still had nightmares believing he and the boy were going to drown.

For all of his minor misdemeanours of staffing a dog, socking a police inspector and his use of inappropriate language, that action in the river must surely cancel out all such. Bravery on this scale was awesome and we thank the Lord this well-trained former Black Watch soldier was there. Unlike some of the new breed, he was never the type to stand on the river bank and watch a child drown because of 'Health and Safety Regulations' but again, he knew nothing of that in Korea when the Chinese were attacking in force and killing his comrades! Alba gu Bragh Jock; another of the best.

Addingham Parish Council with Chairman Mr Alan Jerome MBE presenting the author with a watercolour painting by Brian Irving on behalf of the village on his last day of duty. The Chief Constable granted his authority for the gift saying it was now rare.

Chapter 42

The Force Pipe Band

It was traditional for the larger Scottish Police Forces to have pipe bands and they were a great success with the people in those force areas. Like a football team the locals were very proud of their bands which did much good work for charities and helped cement good public relations.

During the early sixties I put forward an idea for a force pipe band in the White Rose, our force journal. There was some enthusiastic response from a few pipers and drummers but it was not until Mr. Ronald Gregory was appointed Chief Constable that anything further was done. He thought it a good idea for police public relations, a subject that needed constant attention and a meeting was held with him present and we were given the go-ahead to get it started.

To raise funds some of us did private piping engagements, the Scottish Police surgeon gave his fees from private consultations and gradually we built up a fund. Seeing that we meant business we were given a loan which we paid back from our band fees.

The Pipe Major was John Gilchrest a driving instructor with Road Traffic, one time Edinburgh City Police, an excellent piper; his brother Stuart, another good piper was a patrol car driver; Sergeant Batty, P.C. MacAlpine, John Glew, myself and a number of others scattered far and wide about the county made up a full complement of pipers and drummers. Stan Quinlan gave us his blessing but was too involved in fighting serious crime to join the band. He had served as a piper in the Black Watch on the North-West Frontier of India before the separation of that country and was an accomplished piper.

We trained at Dewsbury Divisional Head Quarters in the evening whenever we could attend. Our uniforms came from the Royal Scots Dragoon Guards who were currently top of the Pops with their hit 'Amazing Grace'. This regiment made a great deal of money and were able to change their uniforms more frequently so we got some good kit from them, the tartan being black Stewart. We bought new feather bonnets and paraded for the first time at a football match in Bradford before a crowd of some thirty-five thousand. It went very well. The esprit de corps was excellent; perhaps slightly better than in the general mass of our calling for we were engaged in something different but equally valuable to the morale of the police force.

A Remembrance Parade at Baildon in torrential rain was not ideal. We wore our brand new ostrich feather bonnets for the first time unaware they had been treated with black die. How we played that day I'll never know. The wind was howling a gale and we couldn't hear the orders but we did our best. Because we all faced our front we were not aware of the effect of the rain on the feather bonnets until the parade was over. Oh dear, the dye had run and our faces were streaked black with it. What a mess! We looked more like a carnival band. Fortunately we never suffered so badly from the weather again and looked as we were supposed to, a smart, colourful, harmonious pipe and drum corps.

Attending the practice one evening I noticed Stuart Gilchrist was not looking very happy. Sitting beside him I asked what the trouble was. He explained he'd been on traffic patrol on the M62 when he'd been called to what was thought to be a straightforward road accident. As he drew near the scene he saw a damaged coach and parking his patrol car with the blue lights on he walked towards the coach. Something in the road caught his eye. It was a dead baby. It was then he realised the coach was carrying military personnel and families from Northern Ireland when it was blown up by an IRA bomb.

We were all too aware of the conflict just across the water which was touching most of us one way or another and we longed for it to end. The barracks at Ripon was blown up and selected personnel were given extra firearms training. Many from Ulster moved to stay with relatives in Yorkshire to escape the conflict and the danger, especially the children.

Music is a balm in times of stress and our bagpipe music was no exception and so we played to lift people's spirits' whenever we were requested.

Had the band been established ten years earlier when we were younger its success might have lived on but illness, injury and a little hostility from certain quarters meant its life was short.

We were all under pressure with the 'Yorkshire Ripper' enquiry, investigating those with 'Geordie' accents. The poor Geordies! As if they would have been responsible. Those of us who had considerable experience with mental patients knew exactly the sort of person we were looking for and eventually, after many murders, he was arrested by two patrolling Bobbies and our fears were confirmed.

Because we travelled to Dewsbury for our practice through the red light district of Bradford several band members were interviewed by CID about the murder. One piper was so fed up of this he threatened legal action after the third interview. The whole episode was not the most glorious of the West Yorkshire Police serious crime investigations. We did not expect officers to be exempt from questioning in connection with these horrible crimes but it did give us an insight into how it felt for innocent men to be suspected and how CID were perceived by their colleagues.

For one's name to be put on the list was not pleasant for no explanation was given. One was left wondering if it was someone trying to settle a score or were they just floundering. From our own involvement most of us believed it was the latter.

Band members suffered various ailments from hernias, injured backs, gall bladder problems and stress and with the limited numbers it was the beginning of the end though individuals continued to play privately and still do.

The importance of police wives on rural beats cannot be underestimated. Without them it is doubtful if the system of policing could have worked. Single men living in digs was never ideal but a dedicated man and wife team meant that when the constable was out on patrol his wife was likely at home to answer the telephone or the door to take messages and when serious to pass details on immediately. Callers might appear at any time, day or night and they were never turned away. The position of constable was considered an office, not just a 'job'. It was unique in the establishment structure which might have been its undoing for in administering the law without fear or favour only the Monarch was safe from investigation!

We rarely told our wives anything about our work. They didn't need telling when we had dealt with something sad and unpleasant. They knew but never asked. In a small community things tended to leak out but they remained silent and did not add to the village gossip.

Perhaps the hardest part of policing was tiredness from the constantly changing shift system. This had been the practice from the formation of the police force so the public would never be sure when a constable was on or off duty and regardless of the Constable's needs the beat had to be covered.

Like most birds except owls and nightjars human beings naturally sleep at night. Constables' trying to sleep during the day were constantly disturbed by the telephone, the doorbell or household noises from children.

It has long been known that night shift work is injurious to health over long periods and tiredness does lead to all manner of calamities.

It soon became apparent due to split shifts and the uncanny occurrence of incidents happening towards the end of a shift that a social life was doomed. It might be a road accident or someone dropping dead at the bus stop or any number of things which could not be ignored. In the end the 'job' became paramount and we settled to the life we had been given.

As retards telephones there was one outside in the police office doorway, one in the office itself with extensions into the hall in the house and another at the top of the staircase outside the bedroom door.

Desperate for sleep after endless disturbances I deliberately did not switch the phone through to the house. This was the one and only time I ever did this and it landed me on the carpet.

Up on the A1 motorway a traffic patrol stopped a man and after checks found he was wanted on warrant. Now the only man in the whole of the country who knew if the warrant had been executed was me. I had in fact sent the warrant back without tracing the man. I did not hear the phone and attempts to speak to me in the night naturally failed but I got a ticking off. The uninterrupted sleep was likely worth it!

With the passage of time and experience we became adept at dealing with ever kind of incident from minor matters to the extremely serious. With miles of trunk roads running through the beat road accidents were common for the roads at that time were built for horse-drawn traffic, now much improved. A collision took only seconds but then followed the interviewing of witnesses and taking of written statements. If someone was at fault a prosecution file was prepared by the constable attending and this could take hours, sometimes days if it was a fatal. We did our own typing and the standard had to be very high before it got to the lawyers. Fortunately, I had learned 'touch typing' during my probationary period. Like sudden deaths, road accidents tended to come in threes.

 The key holder of the Memorial Hall rang my wife to say she was unsure she had locked the door to the hall after a committee meeting and would my wife check for her. It was turned 1.0 a.m. as I passed the Fleece and saw this lonesome figure approaching past the War Memorial which seemed slightly familiar. I was in cape and helmet, and having learned the purpose of her walking the street at that hour I accompanied her when a car pulled up. It was a police superintendent from North Yorkshire who had strayed over the boundary. He didn't know me but he knew I must be the local bobby. He leapt out of his car in a flash and rushed towards us.

"Do you need a hand with her Constable, "asked the Superintendent assuming my wife was a prisoner? I thanked him, explained the position to which he seemed unconvinced. He drove off scratching his head. I really think he was disappointed at not being able to assist with an arrest, even if it was my wife. I wouldn't care but she didn't even have the handcuffs on so why he thought she was a prisoner I can't imagine!

When farmers called for movement licences for their stock and had to be admitted to the living room when we lived in Bolton Road the strong smell of cows, sheep or pigs indicated which branch of farming had called. In consequence the door and windows were opened wide and the air freshener used liberally.

If there was a nuclear test on the warning system and I was otherwise engaged the wife had to listen to the signal and record the secret code.

On opening the door one evening a man fell inside unconscious on the floor. That was a bit of a shock for her but calmly she sent for an ambulance and he was safely taken to hospital.

Tramps called now and again, usually wanting a drink of water or directions to the Rectory in the hope the Rector would ease their burden. One such called when I was not there with such a request and told my wife she was very brave. On my return, after he'd gone, I checked him out and he was a very violent, disturbed individual, and yes, she was very brave.

One night when we were both in bed asleep a great banging awoke us from the landing window. It was a young woman who had returned home late up the village and as she was about to enter a narrow ginnel a man lurched out. She ran to us seeking sanctuary and climbed up a high fence onto the outhouse roof to wake us up. She did that alright, nearly giving the pair of us a heart attack. We still have a laugh about it for isn't that what teenage girls are likely to do when frightened?

One dark winter's night a coach pulled up outside and a crowd of young people gathered at the door. It transpired the coach had braked suddenly and several passengers had suffered cut heads from the glass covers over the lights. It was not life threatening but they were shocked and the whole coach load needed the loo. They wore a path up the stair carpet to the bathroom then we provided them all with tea and biscuits. It had been a Jewish outing from Leeds and they were a delight to assist though their Hebrew was little better than mine!

Accident victims were frequent guests especially in inclement weather such as heavy snow when Addingham Bank would become impassable. What else could be done; there was nowhere else for them to go. It was the same with relatives of mental patients who had been sectioned. They often remained with my wife in a distressed state for hours but she did provide that necessary comfort they desperately needed.

On the subject of mental patients! It is said one in four of the population will suffer some such ailment. The police are more and more obliged to lock up sufferers for there is nowhere to send them since the psychiatric wards were closed down and this is a disgrace. Illness can hit any of us and I have known many depressed and stress-hit police officers. As I said before they are not Supermen but they do deal with some of the most depressing incidents that society can throw at them and we all have our breaking point!

The discipline code was strict and we were ever conscious of it. If someone came to the house to report something they had to be attended to for we were never 'off duty' even on rest days and annual leave. To refuse could mean 'neglect of duty'! I recall one man being disciplined for not wearing his hat in the street. He was transferred to another town with all the upheaval that caused but he had been warned!

Piping in a former stately home for a dinner of 500. Fees in those days went to the West Riding Police Pipe Band than later to Help for Heroes.

Chapter 43

A Few Thoughts and Suggestions

Of necessity, not everything has been included in this little volume of social history concerning policing. In the town there was usually assistance not far away; on the rural beat you were on your own and for years there were no radios or transport but we were fit. Nor did we get overtime pay, just time off when the exigencies of duty permitted, which they rarely did. That time was discounted at the year end and seen as for the Queen!

With the reorganisation in the 1970s two officers were taken from the beat and transferred to the town. Also my transport was taken for use elsewhere so I was back on foot, working alone, making out my own shift duties which I did for five years until I suffered injury from a fall in the snow which led to complications and early retirement.

So beat officers were withdrawn, rural stations were sold off or demolished and 'make believe' police with no powers occasionally appeared to drive home what the public had lost. Then, they too disappeared, presumably out of embarrassment for that is how they were viewed!

Sometimes, even Governments have to admit they make mistakes but mistakes can be reversed and the prevention of a completely ungovernable nation is surely paramount for without law and order, everything tumbles down – even Parliament, What good are our Trident submarines if the core of the Nation is rotten with wrongdoing? Quality costs money but from my experience it is worth that expense. The Police are the lubricant that permits all the wheels and cogs in society to function for the common good and what's a few more bob on the rates if it brings back peace of mind and a populace that is reasonably happy?

The name 'Pickles' is from the Norman French and means small landowner which is what I became, returning to beekeeping, keeping hens, geese, ducks and pea-fowl, writing, painting and playing the pipes and violin; visiting schools in poor areas of the city talking to children about the countryside, travelling far and wide to give talks on bees, 'creatures, that by rule in Nature Teach the Act of Order to a Peopled Kingdom' (Henry V Act l). We are that 'Peopled Kingdom'; surely it's worth a try!

We are told crime figures are down. I don't believe it! When there is no easy way of reporting crime because of the unavailability of policemen we do not report crime unless it is very serious and this gives the crime figures the authorities want. In other words policing on the cheap! It seems the police telephone system is designed to discourage calls and is very time wasting if you try to use it.

But it is not just the reporting of crime that is off-putting. What good is a crime number if you know there will be no investigation? Should we really be expected to interrogate suspects ourselves? It could be interesting and some of us would be good at it. I know, for when a former police colleague refused to interview a suspect who had damaged my property because I would not disclose the informant, I managed without the Police and brought an end to the persecution which one must anticipate on retirement if one remains living on the beat! I imagine this is something todays police know little of, living far from their work place, and apart from wearing a numeral, remaining largely anonymous!

In my view, despite higher education, ordinary good manners have deteriorated and the police are not immune! No one knows better than retired officers the perils and stresses today's police face and we sympathise with them. We want them to succeed in the fight against crime; we want to respect them and help when we can but the biggest obstacle is we can't see them because they are no longer there. In Keighley this past two years I have not seen a single officer but I have seen a lot of laws blatantly being broken, enough to give Keighley Court 24 hour shifts if it were still there!

Lord Trenchard, former head of the Royal Air Force, when he became Commissioner of the Metropolitan Police was concerned at the length of time police officers served and wanted it reduced to twenty years with a good pension, the reasoning being that men have given their best years by then.

Provided it is possible to recruit men and women of the right calibre perhaps that is not a bad idea and so far as university graduates are concerned, I have known a number of educated idiots in my time and as Sergeant Tom Haigh used to say of the police, it's like a glass of ale, the froth always rises to the top. Perhaps he was joking for he became a Chief Inspector.

University graduates were comparatively rare then; now as common as blackberries in summer but has original thought suffered in consequence? Both Churchill and Montgomery never attended university and struggled to be admitted to Sandhurst yet they had the 'original' thought, cunning and spiritual faith to see this country through the hardest times. I sometimes think too much education of the wrong type, brainwashing or indoctrination in a particular school of thought can be a great handicap to any student! It no longer seems to come naturally for people to think for themselves as they consult the modern 'oracles' of mobiles and computers!

Policing is basically the same old story of the 'good guys' fighting against the 'bad guys' or it should be; the rest is froth wrapped up in endless paperwork and bits of pink ribbon to tie the hands of the constables! They always say the public get the police force they deserve. Perhaps it is only the people who can change it unless their complacency and apathy is so deep that they are incapable! If so they really will get the police force they deserve and Heaven help us!

In my opinion, as a countryman with a lifetime of experience of nature in the raw, it is only fair to point out the basic problems of a modern society. It is this; if you place five bee hives on an acre of land they have a good chance of thriving. If you place a hundred bee hives on an acre of land they will rob and fight each other, will transmit various diseases and die out. Now the bees had a perfect social order 50 million years before we humans appeared on the planet so as regards the ability to survive they have a head start. Most creatures including human beings react in a similar way to overcrowding.

What I'm trying to say is this; these islands are grossly overcrowded resulting in crime and antisocial behaviour. It cannot be changed by conventional methods and the thought of harsh fascist methods would not be tolerated though it has to be said a little element of fear, even in the top schools, goes a long way to keeping order! At the present time there are no police on the beat to say 'no' to the innumerable offenders of the law. The neglect of small offences leads to greater ones.

To prevent the slide into complete anarchy something really does need to be done! The indigenous people of these islands have only this country; they have no other; they fought two world wars to prevent invasion and because of that their descendants hoped for a better future. It seems that has been and gone and many of them have left for pastures new but they are running out of pastures. Keighley is not the town it was and makes some weep to see its distressed state, remembering how it was with a constable on every beat giving that feeling of security. Perhaps the old town is not worth the expense of that security anymore?

The cities have always been a separate issue and perhaps only a Brigade would be suitable for policing them but for the bulk of our towns and villages it would be well worth going back to the old system of village policing for the peace of our land! Better to have half the population reasonably happy with their police. At the moment they get a raw deal for their investment! I remember an intelligence network second to none built up over many years through trust and honest service thrown away to save a few pounds on the rates. Penny wise-pound foolish! You cannot put a value on the sight of a constable on the street even if he appears to be just standing there watching traffic or pedestrians.

It has been said "Laws are made by superiors for inferiors to obey"! That may be but laws must be seen to deter offenders. Once the crime is committed the law has failed its purpose. It follows that the result of law-breaking is followed by rapid detection and a strict regime that does deter others. This is not so easy in a democracy but liberal-minded people have argued about this for years, the jails are full and are no nearer.

In Britain we will go bumbling on policing to the best of our ability in a humane fashion with public consent and scrutiny but please let's have that scrutiny and see our policemen doing what we pay them to do to keep us safe, even if it means looking under stones instead of waiting for things to happen. The right-kind of hunting can be very satisfactory when those cell doors clang shut and another nuisance is removed from upsetting decent people!

Years ago a councillor in Draughton, another village on my beat, complained of the lack of police presence. The Superintendent in Skipton ordered as many officers as possible to converge on Draughton for a day to report anyone for any offence being committed. The Councillor made no further complaints! Perhaps an election was due and he coveted a bit of publicity! It must certainly have backfired when the summonses arrived for the Draughtonites and there is a lesson in that!

On that note I will just say, we all have a vested interest in law and order so try to support your police; they are all we have got and the 'Broken Force' is not their fault for they deal with the 'effects' but who is responsible for the 'causes'?

Tranquility

CONCLUSION

It was a pleasure to serve the fine people of Keighley and Wharfedale in those twenty years. Many still say they wish they had the police back! I can understand why.

For any aspiring constables who might be reading this I quote a saying passed to me when I was starting out by Mr McDonald a senior officer in the Met, a highlander who had worked in London all through the blitz who went back to the family croft on retirement. He said this: "Do right and fear no man!"

It is good advice to live up to and when the 'underworld' and common mischief makers attempt to sully your name just for doing your duty in serving the people and the Crown you will know your conscience is clear and you will have nothing to fear. Such people will have their reward; it never fails but so will you if you deliberately transgress!

This book could have been written by many constables throughout the country for it is typical of how it was and how the public perceived it. When I hinted I would write a book one day Mr McDonald said, "Don't put everything in it"! I heeded his advice.

Early in my service I was warned to guard against becoming a callous cynic because of the work we had to do. I am glad to say I never did!

Good luck you men and women who carry on the proud tradition. Despite the failings of the system your role is vital to everyone's welfare so take comfort in that; stay safe and when you retire, write and tell us about it. With grateful thanks 295!

The End

INDEX